The House of the Good Spirits

Donn Kushner's books for young people include:

The Violin-Maker's Gift
Uncle Jacob's Ghost Story
A Book Dragon

The House of the Good Spirits

Donn Kushner

LESTER
&ORPEN
DENNYS
PUBLISHERS

FIRST EDITION

Canadian Cataloguing in Publication Data

Kushner, Donn, 1927-
  The house of the good spirits

ISBN 0-88619-288-9 (bound). - ISBN 0-88619-290-0 (pbk.)

I. Title.

PS8571.U82H6 1990   jC813'.54   C90-093843-9
PZ7.K8Ho 1990

The Publisher wishes to acknowledge the assistance
of the Ontario Arts Council.

Jacket design and illustration by John Dawson

Printed and bound in Canada

Lester & Orpen Dennys Limited
78 Sullivan Street
Toronto, Canada M5T 1C1

"Look on the rising sun: there God does live
And gives his light, and gives his heat away;
And flowers and trees and beasts and men receive
Comfort in morning, joy in the noonday.

"And we are put on earth a little space,
That we may learn to bear the beams of love;
And these black bodies and this sunburnt face
Is but a cloud, and like a shady grove.

"For when our souls have learn'd the heat to bear,
The clouds will vanish; we shall hear his voice,
Saying: 'Come out from the grove, my love & care,
And round my golden tent like lambs rejoice.'"

Thus did my mother say, and kissed me;
And thus I say to little English boy:
When I from black and he from white cloud free,
And round the tent of God like lambs we joy,

I'll shade him from the heat, till he can bear
To lean in joy upon our father's knee;
And then I'll stand and stroke his silver hair,
And be like him, and he will then love me.

from "The Little Black Boy"
by William Blake

For the memory of Sylvia,
and for Bill

Contents

CHAPTER ONE

By Wide Waters

From where he watched, Amos thought, the old house looked like nothing so much as a tall ship. The shadows of moving leaves on its walls could have been waves or spray. The great maple tree that overshadowed its roof might have been a mainmast, and the smaller maple behind it another mast—the mizzen-mast, was it called? The flat peak of the roof, with its iron railing, could have been the ship's bridge. He almost expected a captain to appear on the roof, grasp the railing, and stare out over the big lake. Would the ship set sail without him?

It was lucky Naomi wasn't here. Though Amos had never seen her afraid of anything, she *had* disliked her first sight of Lake Ontario.

She and Amos had seen it first yesterday, a long, long day at the very end of summer. They had all flown to Toronto from London, leaving early in the afternoon and arriving just two hours later the same day. Amos knew from his geography book that they would gain five hours of daylight in travelling west from England, in the opposite direction from the turning earth. He explained about time zones to Naomi, when she wondered why the sun was setting so slowly. "What will we do with those extra five hours?" she asked.

"We can get to where we're going by daylight," Amos's mother told her.

Naomi nodded, still not convinced. "Wherever *that* is."

They came into the Arrivals Hall at the Toronto airport in a row: Amos's parents with only three suitcases on one cart, so they could see who was meeting them, then Amos and Naomi with the rest of the luggage on a second cart, with the squashy leather bag from the village almost ready to fall on Amos's head. As soon as that bag had come off the carousel, Naomi had found her long robe and her bright blue and gold headcloth and put them on to enter the new land.

A young white man was waiting for them just outside the Customs door. "Dr. Okoro, and Dr. Okoro?" he said with a little laugh, shaking Amos's mother's and father's hands at the same time. "You're not late at all! You didn't have any trouble with Immigration?"

"The papers were all in order," Amos's father said.

"Of course! People with *your* qualifications wouldn't have any trouble getting into the country, certainly not for a year's stay. Coming straight from London, after all! My name's Bidcup, by the way: Stephen Bidcup."

Stephen Bidcup, Amos said to himself, fitting the name to the man's face. Stephen Bidcup was already losing his hair, except over the ears, where two thick tufts stuck out like horns. His bright blue eyes shone with added welcome. How could he be so pleased to see people he was meeting for the very first time?

Amos's father shook his hand again. "You were very kind to meet us, Dr. Bidcup."

"*Mister* Bidcup," the young man said proudly. "I'm Dr. Baillie's admin assistant. I take the weight of the Developing World off his shoulders, as it were. That is,

I look after some of the details of the exchange program. Including getting you settled."

"It was so kind of you to meet us," said Amos's mother.

"It's my job. And it's often less trouble in the long run. Why, one of the visiting doctors—not from Nigeria, of course—insisted on buying a car as soon as he landed, and we didn't find him for a week. Fortunately, we knew the names of some of his relatives in Hamilton, and we finally located him there."

Amos's father said, "Well, *we're* here, right on time."

Amos's mother nodded. Naomi said, "I'm sure he was happy to see his relatives in Hamilton and they were happy to see him, so far away from home."

Mr. Bidcup looked at her, startled, then smiled. "Of course," he agreed. "And are you with the doctors Okoro as well?"

"This is my aunt, Mrs. Obi," Amos's mother explained.

"Splendid!" Mr. Bidcup leaned forward and shook Naomi's right hand, drawing it away from the bag on the luggage cart. She reached over quickly and steadied the bag with her left hand.

"And our son, Amos," his mother said. "We wrote to Dr. Baillie that he'd be coming too."

Mr. Bidcup shook Amos's hand. "Everything's arranged for you, young man. We've put you down for the Whiteside School. I know you'll find it a friendly place."

Amos's mother beamed. Naomi said, "I hope it will also be a place where he can learn."

"Naturally," Mr. Bidcup answered, looking at her again quickly. "He'll find he has to—that is," he corrected himself at once, "it's a very good school." He glanced at his watch. "Now, I have the hospital van parked in the garage. I'll just bring it to the door, so we can get the luggage in."

"We'd like to change some money," Amos's father said.

"The money exchange is just down the hall," Mr. Bidcup told him. "I'm going that way now." He started off, then stopped. "Are you sure you'll be all right here?" he called back to Naomi.

Naomi pulled the luggage carts together and stood beside them. "I think you'll be able to find me again," she told him.

Mr. Bidcup, followed by Amos's parents, walked down the long corridor and out of sight. Naomi sat on a bench between the luggage carts. Amos went to the bathroom, then took his camera and sketching pad from his travel bag on the cart and sat down opposite Naomi to watch for his parents' return.

A tall, stout, sharp-featured black policeman entered by a side door and looked keenly around the hall. Amos pointed his camera, then set it down and took up his sketching pad. The policeman smiled at Naomi, and she at him. Amos drew the man's large baton and strong face. The face, he saw, was the same colour as his own hand: the rich brown of dark, shaded soil. There were other dark faces among the people at the airport too, though few were as dark as Amos's family and this stranger.

"Why, it's Old Mother Africa herself!" said a voice behind him. Amos looked back quickly. A pale brown man with a sharp, trim beard was standing behind his bench, pointing a long camera at Naomi. "Look at that headcloth!"

"She's perfect! She's just what you want!" The new speaker was a tall woman who stood at the end of the bench, framing Naomi between her hands.

The photographer lowered his camera. "Something's missing," he said. He tapped Amos on the shoulder. "Is that your mammy?"

Amos shook his head. "Never mind," the photographer told him, "you'll do. Can you just stand by her? And give me that wide-eyed look again, won't you? But first take those glasses off; you look like a little professor." Before Amos could stop him, the photographer had slipped his glasses from his nose to his jacket pocket. "I'll buy you a Coke," he added.

Amos put his glasses back on and looked at the man's fancy camera, with all its numbers and dials. "No thank you," he said.

"What does the gentleman want?" Naomi called in English.

The photographer, the tall woman, and Amos walked to her bench. "Are you keeping records for the Immigration Department?" Naomi asked.

"Oh no," the tall woman explained. "Basil is doing the pictures for an article about new arrivals in Canada."

"Don't worry," the photographer added, "I won't steal your soul."

"Steal my soul?"

The photographer stood back, focusing carefully. "Some of you people think that when a picture is taken, the spirit goes into the camera to make the image."

Naomi drew herself up, providing just the expression the photographer wanted. There was a bright flash. Naomi blinked, then answered with dignity, "This person knows that the spirit is more firmly attached to the body than that. What is it?" she asked Amos, speaking in Ibo, their own language. "Your eyes are as big as half-crowns."

"They don't believe that in the village, do they?"

"Not anyone I know." Naomi nodded at the photographer. "This foolish man thinks his fancy equipment makes him wise. Of course," she added, speaking to herself now, "there are many ways to take a person's spirit from his body. But not with a camera." Then she realized that Amos was taking all this in, and stopped herself.

"What are you saying?" the tall woman asked delightedly. "Is that a spell against evil spirits?"

"Hardly," Naomi told her gently, in English. "Evil spirits are always around; if you got rid of one, there'd be others to take its place."

The woman looked for a moment as if she would ask Naomi to explain. Then the photographer tugged at her arm. "Look, more of them, right off the plane!" Five men in turbans had just emerged from a double door. The photographer skipped off towards the new arrivals, checking his camera settings. The tall woman followed in his wake.

Naomi nodded across the hall. "You'd better pick up your camera before someone takes it."

Amos fetched his little camera, still thinking of the photographer's. Who would steal his? He sat down with his sketching pad, took a pencil from his pocket, and drew the photographer, giving him very long, jointed legs. He wondered if Naomi would talk more about the past. She often did so, without explaining, as if he knew as much about it as she did. "Are you tired, Auntie?"

Naomi's eyes came back to the present. She spoke in English, the language Amos spoke with his parents—and with her too, ever since she had decided to come with them to Canada. "I am tired. But it looks like I'd better keep my wits about me, till we get to wherever we're going."

But she fell asleep in the hospital van long before they passed the city limits. Mr. Bidcup sat in front with Amos's parents, talking about the hospital program and Dr. Baillie's plans. Amos watched the landscape go by, when it finally did turn into a real landscape. The sky, out of the city haze, was a hard, clear blue. The trees were so green that he knew there must be a lot of water in the ground. A few leaves had turned red or gold; the rest were waiting their turn. When he saw the big lake on his right for the first time, he almost poked Naomi to show her, but she was snoring now. "Look, Mom," he called to the front seat, but his mother held up her hand; Mr. Bidcup was still talking. The land rose on his right and hid Lake Ontario again.

Amos closed his eyes. The van swayed, as if he were still flying. He heard his father say, "Now, just what sort of place is Port Jordan?"

"It's only a small town, a few kilometres west of Kingston," Mr. Bidcup answered. "It's taken on life in the last few years, since people can live there and work in the city. A bus goes to Kingston every half hour, so you won't both need a car all the time." Then Amos felt that Mr. Bidcup was nodding back at him. "But the school is in Port Jordan itself; your son won't have to travel."

His parents didn't answer, and in a moment Mr. Bidcup continued. "Another advantage of Port Jordan is that the rents are still relatively low. We were able to find you a much more reasonable house than in Kingston. Several of the doctors from our program are there—the foreign doctors, I mean. In its own way, it's a very friendly little community."

"I'm sure it will be a very congenial place," Amos's mother said. Amos almost opened his eyes to see if Naomi was listening, but she seemed to be asleep, and in another minute he had joined her.

The car slowed, made several turns—almost enough to waken Amos up, but he decided to go on sleeping. He didn't open his eyes until Mr. Bidcup said, "Here we are!"

They were parked before a small brownish-green house under a peaked roof with two low dormer windows. The front door was almost hidden by a deep veranda smothered in vines. "It's like a little jungle," Mr. Bidcup said to Amos. "You'll be right at home here."

They all got out of the van. Naomi rubbed her eyes, stretched, and looked at the veranda critically. "We hardly go out of our way to find the jungle," she said. "But this seems quite acceptable."

Mr. Bidcup looked at her, surprised, but busied himself in opening the door and helping to get the luggage inside. They had hardly got farther than the front room when Amos's father looked at his watch and asked, "Will Dr. Baillie still be at his office?"

"Oh yes, till long past this," Mr. Bidcup said. "But he won't expect you on your first day."

"All the same, we would like to see him," said Amos's father. "Just to pay our respects."

His mother nodded. "That would be proper."

"It's not at all necessary," Mr. Bidcup said. Then he looked at their faces. "Still, if you'd be more comfortable. But what about your son and Mrs. Obi? Would you like to stay here and rest?"

"We'll go look at the town," Naomi said.

"Yes," said Amos's mother, "and get yourself something to eat. Here's some Canadian money."

Mr. Bidcup said anxiously, "Don't forget the address. It's 32 Badger Street. A badger's an animal."

"Yes," Naomi said, "the strong, gruff, helpful one in *The Wind in the Willows*. That's a good name for a street."

For the first time, she smiled directly at Mr. Bidcup. His eyes lit up, and he smiled back. "Yes, of course. Well—are you sure you'll be all right, Mrs. Obi? I certainly hope you'll be happy here."

"Why shouldn't I be?" Naomi said.

"Just leave everything till we get back," Amos's mother called from the van. "Get a hamburger in town."

Naomi shook her head as the van drove away. "My, they don't ever stop going! They must think they have to move as fast as they can to stay in one place. That Dr. Baillie won't go away if they don't see him today." She hung up her coat and headcloth, put a plain blue cloth round her head, and pulled her print dress straight. "We're strangers here," she observed. "We'll just look around quietly at first." She and Amos went off to explore the town, walking downhill towards the smell of water.

After two blocks, Badger Street veered right and changed its name to Pilgrim Street. Naomi wrinkled her nose but said nothing. Soon they crossed Main Street, which did seem to be the main street of the town, with limestone buildings and shops one and two storeys high. One low building had a wooden sign, "Port Jordan Library", hanging over a stone inscription, "Customs House". Opposite this was the tall city hall, like a castle in red granite with flags and towers. A sign on the side read "District Museum".

At the corner of Water Street, on the uphill side of Main Street, a wide limestone courthouse stood within stone ramparts. Behind the ramparts a young man dressed in blue trousers and tailcoat, a white shoulder strap, and a tall blue hat paced back and forth. Through holes in the ramparts a row of black cannon pointed across the street at the new police station.

"Oh, my!" Naomi said. She took Amos's elbow. "Someone must be preparing to make trouble!" She looked at two policemen talking quietly in front of the station. "Why don't they have their rifles?"

Amos saw that the mouths of the cannon were full of bus transfers and pop-bottle caps. He freed his arm and ran up the stone steps to a brass sign on the rampart. "This is an old fort," he told Naomi after a while. "There's a bigger one in Kingston, it says. This one was built afterwards, in 1815, right after the war they had with the Americans in 1812. They put the cannon here to guard the harbour, but they haven't been used for a long time."

Naomi looked at the cannon closely, and sniffed. "They could still shoot. I've seen some as old as these, and *they* weren't used to store garbage."

Amos nodded at the young soldier. "Why don't you ask him if they still work?"

"That child?" Naomi snorted, glancing up briefly. "What would he know? Those policemen had better watch out."

But she followed Amos around the corner of the police station and down Water Street. Suddenly, between two long, distant shores with a small, high island between them, the wide lake spread itself out before them, shining to the horizon. The smell of water filled the air.

Naomi came to a dead stop. "Is it the ocean again?" she whispered.

Naomi had not been at all pleased at the sight of the ocean when they had flown to England. This had surprised Amos, who had already seen that she wasn't afraid to travel. She had no problem with the bus from the village to the city, or in the house of his aunt who took them to the airport; there had been no problem until they were up in the air and over the ocean, when she refused to look out the window. On the flight to Canada they gave her an inside seat. Amos had a window seat and reported on the clouds and the changing colours of the water and on every boat or plane he saw. He still couldn't feel that the water was real: the shell of the airplane blocked it out. But Naomi didn't even raise her eyes. She just sat there looking at her book, *Alice's Adventures in Wonderland*, which she had often read to Amos in the village. She became happy when the clouds covered the sea, and even happier when they were over land again.

Now she seemed to think that the ocean had followed her. Amos touched her hand. "It's only a lake. Lake Ontario. I told you about it."

Naomi nodded. When she had decided to come to Canada, she had told Amos to study the country in his books so that she could learn from him. But still she held back as he drew her across the long boardwalk to the beach. "Such a calm sea," she muttered. Along the beach the water rocked back and forth patiently, a few inches at a time. Very cautiously, Naomi walked to the shore, scooped up some water, and tasted it. "No salt," she agreed. She looked at the lake with kinder eyes.

It was a very peaceful scene. In both directions, the boardwalk followed the sand of a wide bay. On the hilly left-hand point, a new hotel was being built. The right-hand point was level and wooded. Over the branches, the high, square turret of an old brick house with boarded-up windows peeked out.

Some swimmers were splashing near the beach, but most of the foreground was filled with boats: paddleboats with couples or small families; windsurfers bending at every angle; larger sailboats gliding to and fro. At a pier some hundred metres to the right of them, a glassed-in excursion boat was loading up. A sign above it read, "To the Thousand Islands".

"What's that?" Naomi cried.

Past the wooded point on the right a large three-masted boat glided into the bay. Most of its square sails were set, and sailors stood here and there on the masts and yardarms, waving to the shore. As the sailboat made for a pier just past the excursion boat, swimmers and people on the boardwalk began to move towards it.

"Come on, Auntie!" Amos took her hand, but Naomi wouldn't budge. She held him back.

"We'll just wait," she told him firmly. Amos looked at her in surprise.

"They say the slave ships looked like that," Naomi said.

"The slave ships!"

"Long ago. Your many-times great-grandfather saw one close, but he got away; it didn't catch him."

"This one won't catch anyone," Amos told her. "It must be the one from Australia, making the world cruise. Didn't you hear them talking about it on the plane? The man said it came up to tour the Great Lakes and collect enough money to get back home. Come on, let's go see it."

Naomi walked with him, still looking worried, towards the sailing ship. "You can see the name," Amos told her. "*The Flying Koala*. That's a kind of bear they have in Australia. Does that sound like a slave ship?"

"Oh, go on with you—I never said there were slave ships now. Only it's best not to rush into things until you know what they are." Naomi stood with Amos, well back of the sailing-ship pier, holding his arm tight. He looked at her face and decided not to try to get closer to the ship. Maybe it would still be there tomorrow, and his parents would let him go.

The ship sailed off. Someone on the beach said it would take a one-hour trip along the coast, around Amherst Island and back. When the ship had vanished past the left-hand point of the bay, Naomi released Amos and sat down on a bench on the boardwalk.

"I suppose it's a fine-looking boat," she said with dignity, "but that doesn't mean a thing. Lots of the slave ships were fine-looking and had pretty names too. The one that almost caught your ancestor, that almost made you be born on this side of the water—if he had lasted the trip—it was called the *Darling Jenny*. And how do I know? That couple who came back from the

United States to our village a year ago, when you were off in London visiting your mother and father. They said they were curious to learn where they had come from. They were light-skinned, like that grasshopper pointing his camera all around the airport. All their blood didn't come from our country, but some did. And *their* ancestors, who were your ancestors too, who had been kidnapped with their two children so many years ago, they heard the name of the ship from some of the sailors and passed it on. The *Darling Jenny*!" Naomi chuckled. "Seems like the captain or the owner might have named it after his wife. What would she have thought if she'd known what the ship would be used for?"

Amos tapped Naomi's arm. "But what about my ancestor, the one who almost got caught?"

Naomi chuckled again. "I bet your folks didn't ever tell you about him. He was on your father's side, and you know how your father's only interested in modern things. He thinks they'll lead him to the Calabash of Wisdom. Your mother too, but if it had been *her* ancestor, she would at least have told you about it. She has *some* sense left." Then Naomi was silent, thinking about that old story. Amos had to tug on her arm to make her speak again. Before she did, she looked at the peaceful lake, at the small boats zipping here and there and the white children making sand castles.

"What was his name?"

Naomi shook her head to collect her thoughts. "He was called Nweke. That's the kind of name all Ibos used to have, before the missionaries came and we started taking our names from the Bible. Some men caught him with his mother and father and his little brother, who was only a baby. The three of them might have escaped if they'd left the little brother, but they wouldn't do that.

"No one knew where they'd gone. Their house was a little outside the village and the men had burned it, to drive them out. But Nweke's mother's younger sister, Adaobi, had been visiting them and had left just before the men came. She heard the cries and the sound of burning and followed after.

"Adaobi followed them all through the night, and the men, the kidnappers, never even saw her. Oh my, she was dark! As dark as you are—" here Naomi stroked Amos's arm— "darker than me, since my colour seems to fade with the years. Adaobi was like a shadow in the forest, they say. Her foot was so light that the grass didn't rustle under her. She followed those bad men through the forest trails, through the scrub and the grasslands, going softly, softly. Sometimes a kidnapper would look up and say, 'What strange wind is that?' She could hear them breathe, she was so close. And Nweke's parents knew she was there, but they kept still and their eyes told Nweke to be still too."

Naomi pointed to the shore. "She was there, as close as the water is to us now, when the kidnappers sold her family to some white men who took them in a long line, all chained together by the neck, over the hills and down to the sea. His mother carried Nweke's little brother and the white men let Nweke walk beside his parents, figuring such a young child wouldn't run away. What could he do but follow? He tried to hold up the heavy chains so they wouldn't cut into his parents' necks, but he was too short. When he *could* reach the chains, the white men chased him away with their whips." Here Naomi squeezed Amos's arm, in grief for that old time.

"And Adaobi followed too, as close as she dared," she said. "She was hiding in the shadows when they put all the chained people in a barracoon, a wooden pen by the seashore. The pen was inside a stockade of logs with long, sharp thorns on top and black guards with whips all around. She saw the big ship waiting off shore to swallow them up. She scratched a picture of it on a piece of wood to warn us, and we copied that picture later. I've seen it; it always seemed unlucky to me. How could such a thing be lucky, when it took so many away and none of them ever came back? It was like a messenger of death, like Tortoise in the old story."

Here Naomi looked suspiciously at Lake Ontario. "It's quiet now, but too wide! Who can tell what's on the other side?"

"But how did Nweke escape?" Amos demanded.

Naomi shook her head. "Right through the bars of the cage, child! Right through the stockade! Somehow his aunt Adaobi signalled to his parents and Nweke squeezed himself out and slid along the shadows to where she was waiting. And she brought him straight back to their village."

"Didn't they even wait to see the ship sail away?"

"Lord, no! What would be the sense of that? They could only taste more danger and more sorrow. His aunt knew it was goodbye to her sister and her family for ever—but she could bring the oldest son back. That was what she had to do, not wait around until she was caught too."

Off in the distance the *Flying Koala* appeared, masking the small island. "See, there it is again," Amos said. "It just takes people out for a sail and brings them right back."

"Oh, I knew that." Naomi smiled. "The days of the slave ships are past, at least for now." She listened to a new sound. "But my tummy's rumbling. We should go look for some hamburgers."

"I didn't know you liked hamburgers." Amos had risen and was pulling off his shoes to shake the sand from them. A movement on the right-hand point of the bay caught his eye: a tall figure with a fishing rod had stepped out, near the house above the trees, and was looking at him, across the water.

Naomi stood up too. "I ate one in London," she said. "We have to move with the times."

CHAPTER TWO

The Rum-Runner

Amos's parents had met as medical students at the University of Lagos in Nigeria's capital city. After they had taken their medical degrees, when Amos was ten, they had worked in government clinics in Lagos. Then the opportunity had come for them to spend a year in London, England—his father at the Institute for Tropical Diseases and his mother at a hospital that specialized in the diseases of children.

These were chances too good to miss, especially for Amos's father, who planned to specialize in tropical diseases when he returned home. But it really didn't seem wise, his mother said, to bring Amos to London with them, to be looked after by whatever kind of help they could find there. She and his father could hardly give him the time and attention he needed while they were studying in the evenings, and even less when they were on hospital duty.

In Lagos they had had no trouble in finding a housekeeper, especially after Amos started school. But they couldn't leave him behind with a housekeeper when they were going as far away as London. And while it was true that his father's parents—who had not really approved of a daughter-in-law with a separate profession—lived in Lagos, they were getting older now and wanted time to themselves.

So finally Amos was sent to what everyone called "the village", really a market town of a few thousand people, where his mother had been born and where her Aunt Naomi, Amos's great-aunt, still lived. Naomi was the widow of a schoolteacher, and a comparatively well educated woman. She also had a store of strange knowledge: you never knew what she would say next. It was not at all, Amos's mother explained to their new friends in London, like leaving their son with ignorant people.

Amos had stayed with Naomi for that whole year, except for two weeks he'd spent in London. Even then, his parents were still so busy that they had to take turns showing him around. They had not really had time to explore the city, but he had read about London before he came. He got them to take him to the Tower, and the waxworks museum, and the big science museum in Kensington. His mother saw the Changing of the Guard at Buckingham Palace for the first time when she took him there.

He brought back a map of London to the village and traced out the places he had visited for Naomi. She followed the route with interest, remarking that in such a big city, in such spiderwebs of roads, there would be plenty of places to hide.

Then Amos's parents received appointments to spend a year in Canada in a fine hospital in the university city of Kingston, on Lake Ontario. His father would be a resident in surgery and his mother in diseases of teenage children.

This time, of course, Amos had to come along; there was never any doubt of that. They learned that he could go to a very good school in Canada, much better than the one he had attended in the village.

Then—Amos wasn't quite sure how it happened—it turned out that Naomi was coming with them too. Her children were all grown now, and gone from home; her last son had left that year. "And you'll need *someone* to look after you," she said. "Your mother and father will have too much to do with their studies to worry about you and the new house both."

In her mind, it was all settled. Amos was more doubtful. He had been reading about Canada in the village school library ever since he'd learned he was going there. He couldn't imagine what the snow and cold would be like, nor the people. He worried more about them than about the weather, even though he had heard that Canadians were supposed to be calm and kind. He told Naomi about the winters: that the ground would disappear under snow for months, and that the lakes and rivers would be frozen solid. She said, "Oh, my!" but didn't seem to be as bothered as he had thought she would be.

"Will we see those big white bears, too?" she asked, looking over his shoulder at a picture in a book.

Amos read the caption to make sure. "I don't think so; they're only near the North Pole. We'll be in the south, near the United States."

"Too bad," said Naomi. "I wanted to see them."

Amos decided not to worry any more about how she would handle life in the new land.

He wished his parents would stop worrying too. He heard them talking in the dark in the small room they were sharing, the night before they flew to Canada. "I just couldn't say no," his mother whispered. "She seemed so determined when she wrote, and it was the same on the telephone; she does have a way with her. But I ask myself, how will she get along with all those strange white people? She's never been outside her village."

"She'll manage," his father said. He added sleepily, "But she did leave the village. Didn't she and her family go into the bush for months during the war? They all came through safe enough."

"Shh!" his mother whispered. "Don't talk about that. Amos might hear you!"

From her tone, Amos knew they were speaking of the big civil war that had been fought in Nigeria a few years before he was born. His parents, who were both from prosperous families, had been able to leave the country during the worst of the fighting, but they still didn't like to talk about it. Amos had learned much more about the war from Naomi: he knew that their people, the Ibos, had tried to set up a separate country called Biafra, and had been conquered. The village had been in Biafra, and people there still talked about the bad times when the government troops came in. Although Naomi's family had retreated into the bush, her husband—Amos's great-uncle Joshua—had been killed by government troops. Naomi had told him all about it—in fact, sometimes she talked to Amos about those bad days as if he had been there too. She had been so brave, he thought. Would he be as brave, in bad times?

His parents began to whisper again. His mother yawned and said, "I suppose she's been through a few things in her time. But still, she was in the country, not in a big city."

"Besides," his father said, "she wants to tend the house in Canada."

"That would be useful. But it'll all be so new to her. She can't drive a car. How will she shop? They say everyone shops by car there. Can you imagine her going to market with a basket on her arm? Or on her *head!*"

"She'll manage," Amos's father repeated, and fell asleep.

Naomi did manage to find a market within walking distance, on the very first day, as they returned to the house on Badger Street. It was a farmers' market, set up in a field between the Roman Catholic church rectory and the United church social hall. She looked with approval at the stalls of tomatoes, peppers, eggplants, and onions, all shining in the sun. She almost crossed the field to a stall full of brown handwoven baskets. Then she shook her head. "Another time. I'd better see to that house."

But she couldn't start fixing up the house that evening. When they returned to Badger Street, Amos's parents were already back, and his mother had made the beds. Though the sky was still light, it was two in the morning, London time. They all slept, though the last thing Amos heard that night was Naomi poking around in the kitchen, snorting at the dirt she found.

Next morning, she really got after the house, scowling at every room. There were cloths and a dust mop in one cupboard, also a vacuum cleaner. After Amos figured out how to use the vacuum cleaner, Naomi tried it on a couple of rooms. Then she ran her finger along the floor, shook her head, and continued with the cloths and dust mop.

The last occupants of the house had left a hamper of dirty sheets and towels; she quickly washed these, using the washing machine. There was a clothes drier too, but she didn't trust it and hung the washing on the line in the back garden.

Then she went out in the garden and began to look it over critically, much as she had done with her own vegetable garden in the village. She shook her head over the tangled raspberry canes, and at the weeds among the tomato plants and the red tomatoes that had fallen from the vines.

She began to ask Amos when school was going to start, in a way that showed she had plans to keep him busy. He had already seen how Naomi had got her own son, a man as old as Amos's father, working around the house in the village. Amos knew Naomi wouldn't hesitate to load chores on *him*!

He thought it was time to go off and explore the town. Maybe the boat from Australia would still be there. No one had actually told him to stay by the house, so when Naomi went to the back garden with the last load of laundry, he slipped out the front door. In a few minutes he was once more by the lakeshore.

This time, as he walked down the boardwalk, a cool breeze was blowing, raising foamy waves. Only a few swimmers were in the water. The Thousand Islands excursion boat was returning, only half full, but the *Flying Koala* must have gone; the dock where it had been moored was barred shut. He continued past the docks, breathing the air from off the big lake, until the boadwalk changed to a concrete path with a dirt track leading off to the left.

A large boulder stood on a rise of ground beside the path, and Amos climbed it to look around. The right-hand path led to the backs of a row of houses and shops on Main Street. Beside a square yellow-brick shop stood a green wooden house, and behind the house was a small vegetable garden with a square of standing corn. In the shade of the corn sat an old man, with the sun shining on his bald head. He was reading a newspaper printed in large black letters in a language Amos didn't know. The old man looked up suddenly, waved at Amos, and smiled. Amos waved back.

Then, as he turned to jump from the boulder, he saw that the other fork of the path led along the shore towards the old house whose upper floor he had seen the day before, above the trees. From the boulder he could see the front of the building clearly: it was a wide three-storey house of faded red brick, much crumbled, with small plants growing here and there from the cracks. A wooden canopy with fancy carved corners sheltered a narrow veranda. The third storey was set back from the others, almost like a tower, and topped with pairs of narrow windows.

The face of the house was dark. Maple trees spread their branches thickly around it, and the vines made only a half-hearted effort to climb the walls. In one corner only, the sunlight shone through a gap where a large branch had been cut off near the trunk. Here the vines grew more freely, in a curious curve, as if the house had a lopsided grin.

But was the grin moving? Were the house walls crumbling? Amos blinked, ready to run. No, he thought, he had just imagined that the house was shaking: it was too solidly planted in the ground.

Or was it? There was that feeling again, that the house was moving, or getting ready to move. That the wind that waved the branches around it would soon sweep the house away, like a sailing ship.

Who could be sailing it? Amos looked up, half-expecting to see a captain on the roof of the house, or sailors clinging to the cornices or window ledges. There was only a shape in a third-floor window that looked like a face; probably just an old curtain or something.

Then the face he imagined he saw—a fat, frightened, drooping white face—suddenly vanished. But how could it? Nobody could really be in the house: the green shutters were closed over all the other windows and rough, unpainted boards had been nailed across them and across the front door as well, so no one could enter. It *must* have been a curtain—but why had it disappeared?

He stepped closer to the house, listening to the creaking whispers of the trees overhead and wondering if there might be another door on the far side that would let him in. Then he leaped back again at the sound of footsteps.

But these were solid footsteps. In a moment their owner walked round the corner, by a flagstone path beside the house. He was a tall white man with a peaked blue fisherman's cap. His thin face sprouted a crop of white bristles. In his hand he held a long-handled net, taller than himself.

He stopped to look at Amos, glancing at his net for a moment as if to see whether Amos would fit into it. Then he nodded his head. "I wasn't expecting company," he said pleasantly.

"Neither was I," Amos said. He too glanced at the net. But the man seemed solid enough—not a fisherman from a strange boat, ready to scoop him up. "Is this your house?" he asked.

The man laughed, looking down at his tattered, worn corduroy trousers. "Hardly mine. You might say it belongs to no one. You ask any of the Murdoch brothers and each one will tell you it doesn't belong to his brothers, though he won't dare claim it for himself. I've taken squatter's rights on the outside, as it were. I'll show you."

With another nod, he led Amos around the house. At the back, facing the lake, was a wide stone terrace with steps down to the yard, then a gravel driveway leading to a black, solid wharf that jutted some twenty feet out into the lake. It was wide enough for a truck, Amos thought, and its timbers seemed strong enough to support one, too.

Amos looked at the wharf, and then at the one by the next house along the lakeshore, near which a small sailboat was anchored. "Is *that* yours?" he asked hopefully.

"Sorry, sonny; not a boat, not a house. But I can *sit* here for the time being." The man looked fondly at the wharf. "*This* was never made for Sunday sailors," he said proudly. "It was meant for real cargo! Even if there's no cargo any more, and no one on it but me these days. But it makes a good quiet place to sit, and fish, and remember."

Amos thought it would be rude to ask the man what he remembered, though he looked as if he had a great deal to remember. But he wondered if he did all his fishing with the long net. "What do you catch with that?" he asked.

"Oh, very special fish," the man said. "Some of them are drying out on the wharf now. I'll show you."

He led the way to the wharf. Two sides of an old packing crate stood at a back corner. Within their shelter, an unpainted rocking chair faced the lake, and the man took his seat on it. "I'm Lester Prewitt," he said gravely, offering Amos his hand.

"Amos Okoro."

Mr. Prewitt nodded. "I saw you yesterday with a lady at the beach."

"That was Naomi," Amos told him. "My aunt."

"I hope to meet her too," Mr. Prewitt said.

He leaned back in his rocking chair, and Amos could see on the railing, by his right leg, a line of curious smooth, twisted wooden figures.

"That's what I catch," Mr. Prewitt explained. "Pieces of driftwood. They're washed up by the wharf; there's a current that sets in to the shore about here. I think it turns inland from Falcon Island. You can just make the island out, as a dot. It's between that big one, Amherst Island on the left, and Adolphus Reach on the right."

Amos focused his eyes and his mind on Falcon Island; it seemed to come closer. Now he could even make out high, rocky shores, he thought, and the roofs of some long, low buildings. He looked back at Lester Prewitt's face. The fisherman was staring out over the lake, smiling at what he saw, but Amos realized that his eyes were glazed with a dull white film. How could *he* see so far?

Lester Prewitt understood his look. "It's all in here." He tapped his forehead. "I see it as well with my eyes closed."

Now he laughed to himself. "Maybe I always could. Once, when my eyes were young, I could see it in the dark from three miles away. At least, it seemed I could, and I needed to be right. Captain Bogart would set me in the front of the boat to guide him around the rocks to the little harbour on the other side of Falcon Island. They said I could see underwater on the darkest night. No matter how much the boat turned and twisted, I had a feeling for that island. Once we were there, we were almost safe home."

"But what was on Falcon Island?" Amos demanded.

"Can't you see? It was a kind of shed, with a house attached. We'd all stop there on the way back from the other side, the far side, where we'd been with the spirits. A lot of boats might be there at once; there was no quarrelling between us on the island, even though we might be ready to trade gunshots on shore. Old Mr. Wagstaff, the one who called himself the Master of Falcon Island, said he'd permit no violence, and what he said went. Sometimes, I thought it was the one peaceful spot in the world."

Amos looked back at the silent house, then again at Falcon Island. "Spirits?"

"Bottles and bottles of them!" Lester Prewitt said happily.

"You kept spirits in bottles?"

At the tone of this question Lester Prewitt turned. He touched Amos on the arm. "Not *that* kind of spirit, laddie," he said with a laugh. "I was referring to alcoholic spirits, mainly whisky and rum. Beer sometimes, though it hardly paid to ship it. You still don't understand?"

Amos shook his head.

"That was more than fifty years ago, when the United States had Prohibition—that meant no liquor was allowed down there. The Americans would pay whatever they had to for good liquor, or not so good, for that matter. But ours was good. The distillers in Toronto would send it down here in trucks, and then where do you think we stored it until it was time to smuggle it across the lake to the States?"

Amos read the answer in Mr. Prewitt's eyes. He glanced back at the house at the foot of the pier.

"That's right!" the old fisherman cried. "This house! The old Murdoch place. It was the only thing the five brothers could agree on, to rent the place to Captain Bogart's boss as a smugglers' cave. If they did agree; likely some of them just decided not to ask questions when they saw money coming into their accounts. Four of them hadn't spoken to each other for twelve years. Once the children of the youngest brother, Angus, hung a swing from the branch of a maple, and in the fall the next brother, Granville, sent a man to cut the branch off. You can still see where it's missing. But they didn't mind sharing the money."

Lester Prewitt wrinkled his forehead. "That may have been an excuse, too. They talked big about who the house belonged to but none of them really seemed eager to live in it. I don't know why. Some say it's a haunted house, but they say that of any old place that's closed up. The only spirits I've seen were the ones in bottles. The good spirits, I called them. I call this place the house of the good spirits. It's my own little joke, though I don't spread it around. Somehow, they still don't appreciate smuggling talk around here. A pious town." He spat in the water.

He fell in with his own thoughts again. "We had a lad like you once; but older, of course. He's no longer with us. Pierre Johnson, his name was; a small part of him was French, though all the French he knew was a few swearwords. Likely some Indian blood, too. His skin wasn't quite as dark as yours, but dark enough to hide him in the night. All but his eyes: Captain Bogart made him wear dark glasses when he sent him to wait for the trucks over on the American side. That was a dangerous job! When the trucks came for the spirits, you never knew who'd come to collect what we'd brought. The truckers might be well armed and not fussy about who owned what. But Pierre Johnson had a nose for trouble; he'd watch and not show himself until he saw how things were. Once or twice he skinned back to the boat and told us to be gone. A brave, cautious man."

He frowned. "Do you know, it was strange: brave as he was—and sometimes it seemed he didn't know the meaning of fear—he didn't like to go into this house here. He'd volunteer to make an extra trip to Falcon Island when the waves were so high we had to sail with half-loads, but he just wouldn't go into this house. Everyone laughed at him for being afraid of an empty house; they said he was still superstitious. But he wasn't afraid. I got the feeling, from what he said once, that he'd decided the house just wasn't *his* place. No, it was the place of someone else. What do you suppose he meant by that?"

Amos shook his head, thinking of the face in the window.

Lester Prewitt said, "Well, if you know, I guess you're not saying. You have a right to your secrets. We all do.

The lake too." He nodded. "It keeps its secrets well. Like Pierre Johnson—it's kept him and his younger brother, who was washed off Falcon Island in a storm and never found. And Pierre's boat as well—the *Shulamite*, he called it.

"That was a story. Pierre saved and saved for that boat, and got it at last—and a fine boat it was. But he couldn't get a crew. A lot of the folk here didn't want to work for a black man. Pierre said the Devil would help him sail it if no one else would. But if he trusted the Devil, he made a mistake. He took a load out alone one stormy night, and all they ever found was a few planks and a life-preserver."

Lester Prewitt grew more cheerful. "But sometimes the lake sends its secrets to shore. Look what it gave me the other day."

He opened a cardboard box to show pieces of dry, very dark wood. "I got these a month ago, and I still haven't figured out what to do with them. I needed my casting grapple to get them; they were just out of reach of the net. Look." A fishing pole was dangling over the edge of the wharf. Lester Prewitt raised it. At the end of the line, a curious series of hooks hung from a circle of light wire, with lead weights between them. "When I give the line a tug, the hooks close. I take all manner of things from the bottom. Once I thought I might snare some old bottles, so many of them were tossed over in the old days when the patrol boats came too close. But the bottles haven't come. Likely, the spirits are still keeping them down there."

Lester Prewitt peered into the box. "But look here!" He pulled out a brass letter A, about as high as a quarter. "Now, this must have come from a boat: I found it on an old piece of oak."

"Could it be from the boat's name?"

"Yes, but it's too small for the nameplate. More likely it was on a box that held some valuables. Here." The old man passed the letter to Amos. "You take it. It's your initial."

"Gee, thanks." Amos rubbed the letter, making it shine again. Then he remembered what he wanted to ask. "But what do you do with the driftwood?"

"Here." Lester Prewitt rocked forward and stayed there. Amos saw a few carved wooden figures sitting on the railing at his right elbow, all in human shape. There were three fishermen with rods and peaked caps, like Mr. Prewitt's. Then there was a woman looking out under her hand; perhaps, Amos thought, she was waiting for a fisherman to return. There was a child, too, with a bundle in his arms. Each of the three fishermen's figures was shaped to the curves of the original wood. The carver's tools were spread out on the ledge: a pocket knife, a few wood chisels, sandpaper under a rock, a pot of varnish, and some brushes.

Lester Prewitt touched the figures carefully. "They're dry now," he said, "They can go in the box. Come on, Martha." He picked up the woman.

"I work here till it gets cold," he told Amos. "Then I work in my basement in town. My museum basement; by the courtesy of another of your brothers."

Amos wondered who his "brothers" were. He looked back at the house. "You don't work in there?" He saw a padlock on the door. "No, I guess you can't get in."

Lester Prewitt snorted. "That wouldn't keep me out! The hasp lifts right out of the wood. I keep that knowledge to myself, though you can use it if you like. But it would be pushing my luck to go in there. One of the Murdochs, one of the present generation, gave me a funny look the other day. I fancied they put up with me as a kind of watchman here; now I'm not so sure how long they'll let me stay.

"But that reminds me." Mr. Prewitt shook his head. "I have to make my deliveries. Whichever Murdoch comes next will find me gone; maybe then he'll worry about the loss of my free services. Let me tidy up first."

He closed the box with the black pieces of driftwood and put his tools and varnish into another box, which he stored in an enclosed space under the railing. From the same space he drew out a large green, black, and white wooden duck; not his own work, Amos saw, for it was too smooth and motionless, like the factory-made ones they sometimes sold in the village market. Then he carefully put his own carvings in a canvas bag, packing rags around each one. He placed the duck in a paper sack. "Here," he told Amos, "you can carry the duck. It might throw Mr. Stern's granddaughter off the scent—though I doubt it."

Mr. Prewitt led the way back to shore, around the old house, up to the fork in the path. The old man was still sitting by the corn stalks, whose shade had now spread over his bald head. He was reading another newspaper; this time Amos recognized the letters but still couldn't understand the words. As they approached him he folded the newspaper and waved it at them, cheerfully.

"The delivery man!" he called. "You're bringing a friend for my friend now?" He waved his foot, in a red leather slipper, towards a low table. On it rested a pink bottle of medicine, a small bottle of pills, a glass of water, and a wooden duck the same colour as the one Amos was carrying.

"It's here, Mr. Stern," Lester Prewitt told him. "As like as a twin. Even your granddaughter can't tell the difference."

Mr. Stern, his eyes very bright, nodded at Amos. "It's in the sporting-goods store on Main Street I acquired that fine bird." He touched the duck's head with his toe. "We took two of them?"

"Only one that time," Lester Prewitt said gently. "After we talked, I went back for the other one. We have it now. Amos here is carrying it."

Mr. Stern, who had been nodding at Amos in a friendly way, suddenly looked at him more critically. "Amos! This is your name? You know what the first Amos said, the one who was a prophet?"

Amos shook his head. Mr. Stern half rose in his chair, sank down again, and raised his finger. He spoke loudly, in a strange language. Then he added, "That's Hebrew, what he spoke. It means: the Lord said, 'I've known you best of all the people on earth, so I'll *really* punish you for your sins!' That's what he said: 'Because you are *my* people, I get to kick you in the *tuchiss* when I like.' In the *tuchiss*, that means in the bottom. Is that a way for a prophet to talk?"

"*I* never said that," Amos protested.

"That's right, Mr. Stern," Lester Prewitt put in. "The boy's not to blame for the name they gave him."

"None of us is to blame," Mr. Stern said. "But you seem like a nice boy. You're bringing me my new medicine?"

Puzzled, Amos looked down at the sack he was carrying. Lester Prewitt laid his hand on Amos's shoulder to prevent him from speaking; he peered carefully at the rear window of the house across the corn patch.

"Don't worry," Mr. Stern told him. "She's on the telephone still. I can hear her."

"The quicker the better, then," Mr. Prewitt said. He took the duck from Amos's paper sack and exchanged it for the one on the table.

"*Zehr gut*," Mr. Stern said. "You didn't make the neck too tight?"

"I tested it," Lester Prewitt told him.

"Let's see." Mr. Stern took up the new wooden duck. He listened carefully. "She's still on the telephone, just in the middle of her discourse." He pushed a small peg on the duck's chest, then turned the head and neck together. The top of the body moved aside to reveal a hollow space in which a small brown bottle was nesting. Mr. Stern stopped, raised his head to listen to the telephone voice within the house, took the bottle out, opened it, said a short prayer, and took a very small drink. He closed the bottle, returned it to the hollow space, and neatly turned the head to close the duck's body.

"So I've got my schnapps for this evening; and for a few more," he announced. "You're a good bootlegger! That's what they called them," he told Amos. "Bootleggers, because they hid the liquor in the legs of their boots."

"That was in the United States," Lester Prewitt said. "During Prohibition. We never had to do that here."

"For me, you still have to. If they'd have had a watcher like mine during Prohibition times, you'd all have been out of business." Mr. Stern listened carefully. "She's off the telephone now."

They all fell silent, watching the back door. Then Lester Prewitt swung his head around and whispered, "She's coming by the alley."

The head of a thin young woman appeared over the corn stalks. "Did you want something?" she asked Lester Prewitt in a sour voice. She advanced until she could see Amos too. "Are they bothering you, *Zeyde*?" she asked.

"Not a bit," Mr. Stern told her cheerfully, but this did not sweeten her voice.

"You mustn't make him tired," she told Lester Prewitt. "There's no work for you today. If you want any work here, you have to ask *me*, not my grandfather." She stared at Amos, still not knowing what to make of him.

Lester Prewitt tipped his cap. "I'm just on my way to the market."

"You're one smart feller," Mr. Stern called to him.

The young woman pursed her lips tightly. Mr. Prewitt bowed and walked off, Amos following him.

"I'll see you soon," old Mr. Stern called.

"Did you take your medicine?" his granddaughter asked.

"I think so," said Mr. Stern. "No, I think I forgot." They saw his granddaughter holding out a pill to him, which he swallowed meekly.

Lester Prewitt waited until they were on Main Street to speak again. "I certainly never worked for *her*. But I cut the grass sometimes on the other houses. She thinks her grandfather shouldn't associate with me, ever since I brought him back from his walk."

"*Brought* him back?"

"He's a smart man; he speaks all kinds of languages. Who knows where he's been, before he came to earth here? But sometimes, now, he walks off in the town and forgets where he belongs. If he belongs anywhere. I brought him home once, with that wooden duck, the day he was wandering around the sporting-goods store and took a fancy to it. And we arranged this little deal that you saw.

"That's why he called me a smart man: it's the only way he can have his little drink—his schnapps, as he calls it—in the evening. His granddaughter didn't know what he meant; she thinks it's just old men's talk."

They were approaching the farmers' market. "I thought it was smart too," Amos said.

"I learned that one from old Goose Donovan. Goose would buy these big decoys, more Canada geese than ducks, hollow them out, and float them to shore with the current. That was no good for large deliveries, but he had a client on a big estate on one of the Thousand Islands who had a taste for real French brandy. The U.S. Coast Guard used to sail right past his client's dock without ever guessing that those wooden geese were carrying Hennessy Three Star Cognac in their bellies."

"Look!" Amos said. "There's my Aunt Naomi."

They were in the farmers' market now. Naomi, with a full wicker basket on her arm, was standing by a vegetable stall talking to a slim, smiling black man in a checked shirt and blue jeans.

"So it is," Lester Prewitt agreed. "She's with Mr. Hicks; he looks after the museum, where I usually sleep. I'd introduce you and make your aunt's acquaintance, but I have to get these carvings to the stall. One of the handicraft people said she'd try to sell them for me. I tried some at the boutique on Main Street, but they didn't sell many there." He held out his hand. "Glad to have met you. Come around any time—until they drive me off my wharf."

"You come to our house, too," Amos told him. "It's 32 Badger Street. And you can bring Mr. Stern, if he doesn't know where to go."

Lester Prewitt nodded gravely, then set off towards another corner of the market. Amos saw that Naomi was saying goodbye to Mr. Hicks. He wasn't sure if she had seen him; when he came up to her, she was examining rows and rows of purple eggplants. The basket on her arm was full, and she stepped aside to reveal a cardboard box under the stall full of paper sacks of vegetables.

"I guess you came to give me a hand," she told Amos without looking up. "I thought you might pass this way, back from the waterside. I timed it just right, didn't I?" She gave him a sweet smile, laid down the basket, picked up the heavy cardboard box, and loaded it into Amos's arms. "That should keep the house supplied for a bit. *Now* we can go home."

CHAPTER THREE

The District Museum

"You might like to talk to that Mr. Hicks," Naomi said. She had set such a smart pace that Amos had to trot to keep up with her. He thought of setting down his box of vegetables, but Naomi gave him a look; then she slowed her walk until he caught up. "I was telling him how you liked to read about where you were and where you had been, and he said you could come see him. He'd have more than enough to tell you." Naomi rolled up her eyes as she said this, and Amos remembered that she had shaken her head after Mr. Hicks turned away.

"I know about him," he said. "He works at the museum."

Naomi started to ask how he knew, but only said, "When you meet him, you'll know lots more about him. He's fond of his own voice. But he has something to talk about, too. He says this town was first settled by black slaves who escaped across the big lake. Canada got rid of slavery long before the United States did, he says, and they didn't need a big civil war to do it. Don't look so surprised," she added. "We haven't seen many black people, but there were lots at one time."

A horn sounded. Amos looked back as a small blue automobile stopped just behind them. "Look!" his mother called from the passenger seat. "A Ford Escort, just two years old. They had it ready for us!"

"It was from Dr. Hassan, who went back to Egypt," his father said. "Mr. Bidcup arranged this, too."

Amos circled the car, looking at his own reflection in its surface. He set down his cardboard box. In the thin layer of dust on the right rear fender he drew a picture of Mr. Bidcup's face, with the two tufts of hair protruding like horns. He looked at the picture and made the horns longer. He heard Naomi chuckle behind him.

"But why are you carrying all that?" his mother asked. "You should have waited for us."

Naomi winked at Amos before he could remind his mother that they had only just learned about the car. His father got out and opened the trunk for his box and Naomi's basket. "Did you bring that basket all the way from the village?" his mother asked suspiciously.

"No indeed," Naomi told her. "I bought it here, at the market. There's a lady who lives in the country, behind here, who weaves them. She has good sense: her baskets hold enough to carry, but not too much, to make a person tired."

Amos's mother nodded. "Well, all right, if that's what people use here. But we can certainly take you shopping in the car."

Naomi smiled. "Next time I'll be sure to wait."

Amos's father looked at his watch. "We have to get back for the conference."

"That's right," his mother said. "We still don't know which doctors we'll be working with," she explained to Amos. "Dr. Baillie's in charge of the whole program, and Mr. Bidcup has been introducing us around. We'll soon know our exact places."

"Now that we have a car, we'll find a little time on the weekend to look around the neighbourhood," Amos's father said.

"Yes," said his mother. "I was feeling guilty about the two of you being stuck here, not able to get around."

Amos and Naomi exchanged glances. "I've already gone quite a ways," Naomi said. "Amos too, I believe."

"How far can you go on foot?" his mother asked. "But we can take you home now. Tomorrow's Saturday. We'll have some real time to see the country then."

As it turned out, his parents did not have much time. They had the house to see to first; they had certainly never planned to leave *all* of it in Naomi's hands, his mother said. They had already discovered a small room beside their bedroom, with an old kitchen table and shelves full of magazines. It would make an excellent office for one of them, once they had cleared out the magazines and found a proper reading lamp.

Moving the magazines to the basement and finding the lamp in a shop on Main Street took most of the morning. Since they had to be back at the hospital that evening, there was no time for anything but a drive through the town and a picnic at the beach. They circled the farmers' market without stopping, and drove along the western part of Main Street. Amos recognized the yellow-brick shop behind which old Mr. Stern had been sitting. He looked between the buildings to catch sight of the old house by the lake. "Driftwood Fashions," his mother said. "They have some nice clothes there." Amos looked back at the shop, but only saw a flash of red and gold in its window.

Main Street continued as the highway west, lined by a row of used-car lots and gas stations. Amos could still see the lake, but when the road left the lakeshore he was glad his father turned around. They drove to the centre of the town and parked near the beach.

Naomi had stayed behind to deal with the house, even though both of Amos's parents had urged her to come along. "Besides, you all have to get acquainted again," she had said to his mother, who looked surprised, then smiled.

"I guess you haven't found much to do around here yet," she said after lunch, as they sat on the lakeshore. "But school starts on Tuesday, after what they call Labour Day. Oh," she added, raising her voice so that his father, who had been sitting aside reading a reprint of one of Dr. Baillie's scientific articles, could hear too: "That Mr. Bidcup. I learned yesterday that his wife is the vice-principal of the Whiteside School, your new school. Isn't that fine? I'll take you there Tuesday morning. She's looking forward to seeing you, Mr. Bidcup says."

Amos made a face. "Well! You don't have to be afraid of school," said his mother. "Everyone has to go to school. I'm surprised you don't like it."

For a moment, his father's head left the article. "You must have had it too easy in the village. I just hope you won't have any trouble now."

"I know you kept up your reading," his mother told him. "If you pay attention, you should do well." She looked at his father, who had volunteered to repack the picnic basket but had gone back to reading his article when the basket was still only half-full. She coughed; his father put down the article and turned to the basket. His mother looked at Amos, who was gazing across the water. "There's so much to do," she sighed. "So much to learn. We don't want the people here to think we're ignorant. They seem to know everything. We could spend all our time at that university library and still not catch up. I had to persuade your daddy to come out here today, so we wouldn't go on being strangers to you. He wanted to study; he's still studying."

"Does he want the Calabash of Wisdom?"

"The what?" Then Amos's mother smiled. "That old story! I'd forgotten it." She looked dreamily over the lake. The wind had died down and the waves made only a soft, nuzzling, sucking sound. "Such a still lake. It's like the sea, but so peaceful." She looked along the boardwalk and at the backs of the wooden houses towards the eastern end of Main Street, where the row of shops ended. "Here too. They must be such calm and kind people here, don't you think?"

"I hope so," said Amos, who had some doubts on the matter.

"It's all ready." His father had got the picnic basket packed very neatly; he always worked neatly when he set his mind to it.

He began to talk about a special kind of surgical retractor used by Dr. Thurgood, the hospital's Chief of Surgery. He'd never seen such an implement before, even in London. But he thought a good mechanic might be able to make a serviceable one out of spring steel.

"Dr. Thurgood?" Amos's mother asked. "Will you be working with him? I thought it was to be Dr. Kalinsky."

"Likely both of them, or neither one," his father replied. "I'm not sure which." This brought him back to his own thoughts, and he drew the article out of his pocket again. "I wish I'd had time to look up the other articles they refer to here. I really should have copied them and brought them home too." He turned his head to look longingly to the east. "Amos hasn't seen the hospital. We might just drive by there and I could dash in to the library and find them while you wait."

"No," Amos's mother said firmly. "I know your 'dashes' into the library—it'll take you a long time to find everything you want. You take the car, and we'll stay in town and walk around some more. Maybe that museum in the city hall will still be open."

Amos's father looked at his watch and clicked his tongue. "The library may be closed! I'll telephone to make sure." The others watched while he walked quickly to a phone booth on the boardwalk, then returned. "I just have time if I leave now."

Amos's mother motioned to him; they hurried to put the picnic basket into the car before his father could drive away. As he backed out, Amos saw that the dust picture of Mr. Bidcup was still on the fender.

He and his mother walked up Water Street and along Main Street to the city hall. His mother was still shaking her head. "Your father worries so. He's fussing about which doctor he'll be working with. And he wouldn't sleep tonight if he was thinking about having to find those articles tomorrow. But I want to relax today, while I still can. Work really begins next week.... Look, I do believe that museum door *is* open."

A sign on the door, in a cobblestoned alley beside the city hall, told them that the museum would close in half an hour. "We'll just have a quick look," his mother said.

They walked up a flight of stairs to a wide room on the second floor, a room divided by rows of display cases that showed collections of medals from the time of the old fort, faded letters that told of the life of the early settlers, and a royal charter that granted land to a Brigadier Archibald Murdoch. Taller cases held headless dummies with long uniforms, striped with silver braid, and ladies' dresses full of flounces and ruffles, from the last century. Along the walls were photographs of settlers and prominent early citizens.

It was strange, Amos thought, that no one else was in this room, not even a guard. A leather swivel chair behind the wide desk by the entrance was turned sideways as if someone had just left, but he could hear no sound of voices or footsteps or breathing. His mother had stopped before a photograph showing rows of stiff, serious teachers and another photograph of even more serious students standing before the white pillars of a small college. She nodded and passed on to a series of photographs of a young lady, born in Port Jordan in 1890, who had become a Hollywood star but had never forgotten her simple birthplace.

Amos called, "Look, Mom!"

He had found a large photograph showing rows of black people, with a bearded black minister in their centre, standing before an unpainted board church. His mother joined him and they examined the picture together. Many of the men were bearded too: solid, stocky figures with hands held stiffly at their sides. Some wore hats, most wore suits, and the minister wore a long frock coat. The women clustered at the sides wore long dresses and seemed just as serious as the men, except for one young woman whose smile—likely at someone behind the camera—lit up a corner of the picture.

Amos started at the smell of peppermint. "Ah!" a rich, rumbling voice said. "You've found one of our most important displays."

They turned to see a portly, white-haired old gentleman with a splendid sweeping white moustache. He wore a rich tweed jacket over a fine orange sweater; as he rocked back on his heels, Amos saw that he was also wearing yellow moccasins, which must explain why he could move so quietly.

The old gentleman slipped on a pair of spectacles from his jacket pocket and leaned forward benignly to peer at the picture of the black congregation. "These good people were some of our finest settlers," he announced. "We're all very proud of them; they came across the lake to a land of freedom. Under the lion's paw, as the fine old expression had it, meaning under the protection of British law."

"Did they build that church here?" Amos asked, before his mother could speak.

"Not exactly here. A few miles back, in the country. For years they had a thriving settlement. They were excellent market gardeners; you might say they served as greengrocers to this town."

He coughed modestly. "I have somewhat of a personal interest in this fair town myself. Have you noted its name?"

"Port Jordan?" Amos said.

"Is it like the River Jordan in the Bible?" asked his mother.

"Nothing so grand as that," said the old gentleman. "An ancestor of mine, one *Jordan* Murdoch, was a very early settler here." He coughed. "The story isn't generally known."

"It was good of you to tell us," said Amos's mother.

Amos looked at the picture again, and at a card beside it on which was typed, in faded letters, "The Ebenezer Baptist Church of Buford."

"Are they still in Buford?" he asked.

The gentleman coughed. "Time dispersed them. Mr. Hicks can tell you more. Hicks!" he called, "Oh, Hicks!"

"Yes, Colonel," a soft voice replied. The slim black man Amos had seen with Naomi at the market the previous day appeared before them, so quietly that Amos looked down at his feet—but he was wearing hard shoes instead of moccasins like the old white man.

"Our visitors are interested in the Buford Settlement," the old gentleman announced. "Perhaps you'd care to tell them about it."

"Certainly." The black man smiled at Amos and his mother. "My name is Cecil Hicks," he told them. "I'm the curator of this museum."

Amos's mother shook Mr. Hicks's hand. "I'm very glad to meet you, sir. And you too." She turned to the old gentleman. "Mr...."

"This is Colonel Murdoch," Mr. Hicks said. "Of one of our founding families."

Amos's mother held her hand out to the colonel, who shook it, surprised. "Are you with the museum too, Colonel?" she asked him.

The colonel cleared his throat. "Only in an unofficial capacity."

Mr. Hicks said quickly, "Colonel Murdoch has been Secretary of our Board of Governors. He likes to keep an eye on us."

"I am *Honorary* Secretary," said the colonel. "After long years of service." He shook his head, suddenly puzzled. "Do you know, the land on which this very building stands"—here he struck the floor with his moccasin—"was given to the city by my grandfather. He had it under a royal charter." Then he walked to a showcase. "This brooch belonged to my great-aunt Clementina Murdoch. But where is it? Oh yes, here. And the medals, too: all are family mementoes."

Mr. Hicks nudged Amos quietly. "Would you like to see some of those writings about the early settlers, son?"

Amos nodded.

"Come on," the curator said, "I have them in my office."

He walked towards a door, with Amos close behind him. Amos's mother started to follow but the colonel said quickly, "I noticed you were looking at those costumes, madam. Let me tell you about them. You wouldn't believe how many came from members of my family." He stood by a case until Amos's mother joined him.

Mr. Hicks winked, led Amos into his office, and closed the door. "The colonel's in rare form today," he said. "I hope he won't talk your mother's ear off. But he *can* be interesting if you discount half of what he says."

"Is he crazy?" Amos asked.

Mr. Hicks frowned. "Crazy? Now, that's a harsh word. He's quite clear-headed on many matters. And he really is a colonel—he served overseas in the Second World War. But the more enterprising members of his family somehow cheated him out of his share of the family properties while he was away fighting. They did have a lot of land, though not as much as he makes out now.

"But we were talking about the real history of this place. Wait, I'll show you. Just sit here." Mr. Hicks pulled back a basket chair with high wooden arms from the desk, sat Amos in it, walked into a corridor that led to a second door, and came back with a thick file of typed pages. "This is a history I've written of the Buford Settlement, the one in the photograph. It can't leave the museum. But you could read it here."

Amos looked at the heap of papers in dismay. The sentence his eye fell on read: "These three groups disputed the boundaries of the glebe lands and brought the case to the Circuit Court. Due to their disinclination to consider each others' doubtlessly valid requirements, they expended interminable years in litigation. The minister of one congregation called his clerical adversary 'The Antichrist', and in turn was described as 'The Whore of Babylon', to the scandal of the faithful." He put his finger on the words, to follow them. To his relief, Mr. Hicks closed the file and removed it.

"On second thought, that might be a little advanced," he said. "Besides, it's still not finished. I have more research to do. I'm afraid I lost interest in the Buford group. In any case, they weren't the first black settlers, the ones who really named the town."

"It wasn't named after Colonel Murdoch's family?" Amos asked.

"Of course not. *Jordan* Murdoch indeed!" Then Mr. Hicks added thoughtfully, "I'm tempted to search the records just to find out what sort of rascal this Jordan Murdoch was, if he ever existed. No, we named it."

"Someone in *your* family?"

"Not exactly, no. My ancestors crossed the Detroit River, near Windsor, some six hundred kilometres west of here. It was easy to slip across there, you know; you could do it in a canoe on a dark night. There were all sorts of settlements of escaped slaves in the district. Here's a map I've drawn up; it's still not complete." Mr. Hicks pulled out another file and took out a large map showing Lake Ontario and Lake Erie, with many spots numbered in red along the shores. He spread this out in front of Amos, leaning over him in his basket chair. "Here, and here, and here," he said. "My people crossed here, when it was still easy, before the Fugitive Slave Laws were passed. I assume you've heard about them."

Amos shook his head.

"My," said Mr. Hicks, "what *do* they teach you? The laws were passed in the United States, in 1850. By then the northern states had abolished slavery, and before the laws were passed, any slave who escaped to the north was free. But after 1850, under the new laws, they could be taken back to the south, to their old owners. The slave-catchers—or bounty hunters, as some called them—came north to hunt them down. But if the slaves made it to Canada, which was still really part of Britain then, they couldn't be taken back across the border. Now, this *will* interest you." He began searching the shelves. "I was collecting some notes on the slave-catchers, for an article—what's that?"

From the other room came the sound of the colonel's voice booming, and Amos's mother's polite laughter. The curator listened carefully. "Is he opening those display cases again?" he muttered. "How did he get the key? I'd better see what he's up to." He walked out the door, pushing the chair on which Amos sat closer to the table as he passed him, blocking him in. Amos's feet did not reach the floor, and the only way he could get out was if he climbed over the desk. Instead he found a piece of blank paper on the desk, took out his pencil, and drew a picture of Mr. Hicks hiding behind his display cases, carefully watching Colonel Murdoch. He was so busy drawing the colonel's moustache that he just had time to turn the paper over when he heard steps returning.

The door opened. "All is safe outside," Mr. Hicks said. "That colonel is such a sly one, I have to keep a good watch on him. Rather than look for those notes, I'll make you a copy of my article when it's done. But after the new laws came in, the slave-catchers watched the easy river crossings too closely, so some of the slaves decided to make the trip right across the lake. This was one of the spots—" He pointed again. "Where we are right now. Despite the storms, and the ice in winter."

"But how did the town get its name?" Amos asked.

"I've been telling you. Some of those who made it to this spot named it Port Jordan, after the old song, 'My home is over Jordan'."

"But where did they all go? You're the first black person I've seen here," Amos told him.

"Well, most of them moved away," Mr. Hicks said. "You and your aunt and your parents now bring the black population of Port Jordan up to ten, three of whom are in my family. The others moved up country after a while."

"Why?"

"Well," Mr. Hicks said, "you might say they were *induced* to go. But that's another story, which I'll tell you sometime. Anyway, when they came to Port Jordan, there was hardly any town at all. Only the fort. But there were some black soldiers in the fort, men who had been slaves in the United States. Now, let me show you something else." He pulled back Amos's chair so that he could open a wide drawer of the desk; he drew out a folder with a piece of yellow paper inside it, closed the desk, and replaced Amos and the chair.

"This is a letter the black soldiers wrote, petitioning the commander of the fort for more wood for their fires," Mr. Hicks explained. While Amos tried to figure out the old-fashioned script, the curator leaned over him and read the end of the letter aloud:

> We had thought, before, that we were in the bowels of Hell itself, amid the whips and the mosquitoes of the southern swamps, before we were brought to this free land. Now we ask, to what place have we been sent? Have we come from Hell to Purgatory? We see cold fogs, threatening ice castles on the great waters. Will Spring never come? We are like those dammed sinners, said to be buried in the ice, shining through it like flies in amber. Where is the enemy we are expecting? Is there such an enemy? Are we ourselves God's enemies, and our punishment to come here? Only you can release us from this new bondage.

At the bottom of the paper, Amos read:

> February 12, 1817
> Jefferson White (Private)
> Samuel Musgrave (Private)
> Rufus Palfrey (Corporal)
> Josiah Stone (Private)
> Cyril Wedderspoon (Chaplain)

All the names were in the same handwriting. Beside the names of Jefferson White and Josiah Stone were X's: beside Rufus Palfrey was a mark of two links of chain, and beside Samuel Musgrave a little sketch of a book. "That Cyril Wedderspoon must have been a white man, from England," Mr. Hicks said. "He must have written all this, and the others signed with marks because they didn't know how to write. I think they were slaves who were taken to Canada by British ships during the 1812 war with the United States."

He paused. "Am I going too fast for you? I'm sure you know that during both the American Revolution and the War of 1812 the British government offered freedom to any black slaves in the United States who would join their side."

"No."

"My," Mr. Hicks said, "I thought *everyone* knew that. Well, that's how this group came. They probably joined the militia in Toronto and then were sent to this little fort, where white soldiers didn't want to go. I think the winters were especially cold here, so hardly any white settlers came.

"But the slaves who crossed the lake later, after the Fugitive Slave Laws were passed, didn't know any better—or if they knew, they didn't have a choice. Many came in summertime. A big boatload of them came in 1852. They'd been promised land by the British government, who wanted them as workers, but what they were given was land along the shore that no white person wanted.

"But oh my, they had faith! They had such faith that they built their church on the shore of the lake, on some land they didn't even have clear title to. A wooden church. It burned down one night in 1857, just four years after it was built. There was talk that the fire was set on purpose, because by that time the regular settlers, the people from Kingston, had begun to realize the value of land along the lake. The Murdoch family took the land over and built a big house just where the church had stood. I think you've seen it."

"Is that the House of the Good Spirits?" Then Amos bit his tongue. Perhaps Mr. Prewitt had wanted to keep the name a secret.

But Mr. Hicks didn't seem surprised. "I see old Lester told you its name; he seems to trust you." He was suddenly thoughtful. "Maybe it *is* a house of good spirits, though the Murdoch family has hardly been forthcoming with historical details." Mr. Hicks shook his head thoughtfully. "Yes, that's where the church stood," he continued. "With a tall wooden spire that could be seen from far out on the lake."

"Could they see it from Falcon Island?" Amos asked him.

"Especially from Falcon Island—did Lester tell you about that, too? When the slaves crossing the lake came around Falcon Island and saw that spire, it was like a beacon to them. Many of them knew the name of the church already—the Church of Paul and Silas, they called it." Mr. Hicks paused.

"Were Paul and Silas their leaders?" Amos asked.

"Not really," Mr. Hicks said, smiling. "Though probably some of the slaves thought they were. No, they're out of a Bible story. I came across a sheet of paper from the church itself; it must have been printed by one of the first ministers. I want to show it to you."

He pulled Amos and his chair back from the desk again, opened the drawer, and carefully drew out another brittle yellow sheet of paper. At the top of the page was a picture of a black man with a stick and bundle over his shoulder, standing on the shore of a narrow river and looking fearfully backwards. On the other shore of the river was a black family: a man on his knees kissing the ground; a woman holding a small child with either hand; the three of them watching smaller figures in the distance building a wooden church with a tall steeple.

Below the picture was a text in thick letters, something about magistrates renting garments. But before Amos had time to read it all, Mr. Hicks took the page away. "Maybe you know the old spiritual." Here he sang in a surprisingly quiet, sweet voice, " 'Paul and Silas bound in jail, all night long. One for to sleep and the other for to pray, all night long.' You see, Paul and Silas were bound in jail until an earthquake broke the prison and set them free. The black folk who made up that song had been bound in jail, so to speak, for many years. They were hoping that an earthquake would come and set *them* free."

He walked away from the desk, his eyes dreamy, and stared out at the lake. "And an earthquake did come!" he said.

A gentle tap sounded on the door at the end of the long corridor. Mr. Hicks opened the door and spoke to someone behind it, then closed it softly. Amos had caught just a glimpse of a blue peaked fisherman's cap.

"Was that Mr. Prewitt?" Amos asked.

"The very same; he wanted to see if the coast is clear. I let him keep a bed in the basement. He looks after the furnace in the winter, and shovels the snow, and takes care of the lawn in the summer, for a salary that just lets him stay alive. If the directors wanted someone younger, with his own home, they'd have to raise the pay. So this arrangement suits them fine, and they pretend not to know where old Lester is sleeping. But you can never tell when the colonel's going to start nosing around down in the cellar."

"Is that why he wears moccasins, so he can spy?"

"Probably. But my ears are pretty sharp, and I've kept him under control so far. I'm more afraid he'll make a speech at the directors' meeting that will make them ask what *he's* doing here. This museum is almost his only home, too. He has a miserable room in a boarding house somewhere, that he's ashamed to talk about." He smiled suddenly. "I imagine I'm the only curator in Canada who has two such wounded birds to watch. But I hear silence from the next room. The colonel's probably imparted enough wisdom to your mother for one day."

There was a knock on the door and Mr. Hicks opened it. Amos's mother said, "I'm to remind you it's closing time." She sighed. "Now I know *all* about the first families of the town."

"Not all, Mom," Amos said.

"I look forward to hearing the real story, then. But we'd better be going."

Mr. Hicks looked at his watch. "It *is* closing time. Please come back, both of you."

He opened the door to let them out. "I'll find you a book about that earthquake, too," he told Amos.

"Earthquake!" Amos's mother was alarmed. "Do they have earthquakes here?"

"I meant the civil war, the one in the United States. It really shook things up; they're rumbling still."

"But not here, I hope," Amos's mother said.

"I hope not," the curator agreed.

Amos's mother looked at him curiously as they walked away from the museum. "Was Mr. Hicks interesting?"

"Yeah. I guess so."

His mother touched his shoulder. "You look as though an earthquake hit *you*!"

Amos shook his head to clear it. "Why does everybody want to teach me things?"

"I noticed that in London, too. It's because you're such a good listener." His mother squeezed his arm. "But you have to learn some things by yourself," she added.

CHAPTER FOUR

Escaping in the Jungle

In the next few days, it sometimes seemed to Amos that his own words were waiting to trip him up. The meeting with Mrs. Bidcup went better than he had expected. She was a thin lady, taller than her husband, and in a big hurry this first day of school. But her shrewd grey eyes didn't seem to miss much. "We've all been looking forward to your coming here, Amos," she said. "I've put you in Mrs. Poultney's class, in our fifth grade." Then she looked at Amos very carefully, weighing him with her eyes. "That seems to be the right level. If you find it hard at first, come and talk to me; that's what I'm here for."

His mother looked polite and serious. Amos said, "I can manage the fifth grade. I finished the fourth one at home."

Mrs. Bidcup looked at him as if she would like to talk longer, and nodded. "That's the right spirit." Then she glanced at her watch. "Goodness! The meeting has already started. Harriet," she called to her secretary, "can you take Amos to Mrs. Poultney?"

Then she was out the door. Amos's mother, who had been glancing at *her* watch, left for the hospital.

Mrs. Poultney was shorter, younger, and more worried-looking than Mrs. Bidcup. She was calling off the names of students to a group who were already seated, and who were so busy talking among themselves that they didn't notice Amos as he entered the classroom.

Someone said, "A chocolate bar!" It was a fat, pimply, red-haired boy at the back of the class. Then a thin cold voice said, "Something to add to the lemon drops and caramels." Several children giggled; some turned to stare at two East Indian girls who were whispering together and paid no notice, and at a Chinese boy who was searching for something in his knapsack.

"Be quiet, Norman and Henry," Mrs. Poultney said without looking up. Two girls giggled. "Quiet!" Mrs. Poultney said again.

The class suddenly became silent and all of them looked at Amos as if the next move was up to him. He fidgeted in his grey flannel trousers and blue blazer that his mother had thought proper for his first day at school. All the boys, and some of the girls, seemed to be wearing blue jeans.

Mrs. Poultney picked up a card from her desk and cleared her throat. "Class, this is Amos Okoro. He has come from a great distance and I want you to be sure to make him welcome."

A girl's voice said, "*Bonjour.*" Several students giggled, but no one else spoke.

Mrs. Poultney consulted her card. "He will be richer in some experiences than you and possibly poorer in others. I'm sure we will all have something to learn from each other."

The class took this remark in silence too, and Mrs. Poultney told Amos to sit down at a middle desk. On his right was a girl with long, straight black hair, the one who had just spoken; she gave him a kind smile. Otherwise, as he told Naomi later that day, the students looked at him as if he were some strange animal.

("Humph," Naomi said, "they just don't know what strange animals *are!*")

The class wasn't bad after that. They were just reviewing arithmetic, at a level that Amos already knew. Mrs. Poultney called on several other students to work out problems at the board. Naturally, he wasn't going to volunteer, though he had always liked numbers. This was the time to "go quietly, quietly", as Naomi might have said. He began to work out the problems by himself and grinned when he saw that two of the answers on the board were wrong. Mrs. Poultney was looking at him; he erased his grin and looked down.

"Now, Amos, pay attention please!" the teacher called. All the class was watching him. "We know that this may be new and strange to you," Mrs. Poultney continued, "but you can't learn unless you pay attention."

"Yes, ma'am," Amos said.

Behind him, someone whispered, "You *better* say, 'Yes ma'am,' boy!"

"Norman Glanders, that's quite enough!" said Mrs. Poultney. "Others might not appreciate your so-called humour."

"Yes *ma'am!*" the red-haired boy said.

Mrs. Poultney rapped on the desk just as the bell rang for recess. Most of the class made for the door immediately; one or two glanced at Amos as they passed by. The two Indian girls walked out, talking to each other; the Chinese boy held a baseball in his hand and whistled. Norman Glanders passed so close to Amos that he could smell the red-haired boy's stale sweat. "You stink!" Norman hissed at Amos. Then he grabbed the arm of a tall boy with wild black hair and spoke in his ear. "Indubitably!" was the boy's thin, cold reply. Mrs. Poultney called again, "Norman Glanders and Henry Stiggs! You boys can tell your jokes outside!" The two left, pushing ahead of the others.

Amos followed the class out the door to the rear schoolyard. A high fence of diagonal wire strands extended from one corner of the school halfway down the schoolyard. At the right-hand side of the fence a game of baseball had started, with teams already formed. On the other side of the fence children from the second and third grades, who had left the school by a side door, were playing around a slide and a jungle gym.

Suddenly, the sound of crying came from a group of smaller children gathered at the far end of the fence. As Amos looked, the head of a small boy climbing the fence rose above the others, and the sound of his voice rose too. He continued crying as he climbed, and when he reached the top he clung there, sobbing loudly.

The dark-haired girl who had smiled at Amos stood along the fence, watching. As Amos came up to her she said, "That's Jeremy—he always gets stuck."

"On the fence? Is he really stuck?"

"Frozen. Look at him." At these words Jeremy's cries became louder and more shrill. The catcher at the baseball game looked up, annoyed. Some of the larger children began to gather opposite Jeremy on his fence, laughing.

"You see," the girl explained, "it's curious: Jeremy can climb up, but he can't climb down. The shop teacher, Mr. Cartwright, must bring a ladder to rescue him." She looked across the schoolyard. "I think someone has already gone to get him, but he won't hurry. You are Amos Okoro, no?"

Amos nodded.

"I am Juliette Bellechasse." She looked back at the school door. "Mr. Cartwright doesn't like to climb, you see. I think it makes him afraid."

Jeremy's cries became even stronger, then stopped as if he couldn't breathe. In a moment they started again, but with less breath in them. "Some of the others tried to stop Jeremy from climbing, but he kicked," Juliette commented. "Once he starts to go up, he is afraid to go down. I wonder why."

Amos looked for Mr. Cartwright again, but saw only more children on each side. Norman Glanders and Henry Stiggs were standing near the catcher, both pointing and laughing at the smaller figure on the fence. Amos had been laughing too, but he stopped when he saw them. "Someone should help him," Juliette said.

"Hold this." Amos handed Juliette his blazer. He walked quickly along the fence, behind the catcher. Norman Glanders called, "Hey, jungle boy, why aren't you on the jungle gym?" but Amos had other things on his mind. He ran around the end of the fence and pushed his way through the children who were clustering below Jeremy, until he could grab the fence. Climbing it was hard work, since the toes of his shoes barely fit into the openings between the wires. He thought of kicking off his shoes, but felt how the thin wire was cutting into his hands; his feet needed the protection. He kicked into the fence, so that his shoes could catch better. Jeremy's feet came into line with his eyes, then his scratched legs, then his twisted trouser belt. Then Amos was beside him. "Do you want to come down?" he asked Jeremy.

Jeremy stopped crying. "I can't," he said very seriously. "If I climb down, I'll fall. I fell once."

Amos moved closer to him, then put one leg past him and moved down a few rungs, so that he was surrounding the smaller child. "What you have to do," he explained, "is close your eyes and turn so you can hold onto my shoulders. Then I'll climb down for both of us. Can you do that?"

Jeremy thought about it. "Yes," he said gravely.

"Close your eyes then. But hurry up. And don't knock off my glasses."

"All right," Jeremy said. He closed his eyes, turned, and put his arms around Amos's neck, pushing his glasses to one side. Amos nudged them back into place with his shoulder. Jeremy was very light, he thought. Still, he could feel the extra weight as he lowered himself. It was harder than before to keep his toes in the fence. His mother *would* insist that he wear real shoes today! Running shoes would have been easier. He found that if he bent more in the middle the pressure of his feet against the fence increased, although this also put more weight on his arms. Jeremy still had his eyes closed and breathed so quietly that he might have been asleep.

They were almost down now. Amos took his feet from the fence and landed with a thud. Jeremy opened his eyes, slid to the ground, and scampered away.

Then Jeremy turned and stuck out his tongue. At him? Amos wondered. No, it was to one side. He looked back in the direction the tongue pointed and saw that Norman Glanders and Henry Stiggs had come around to their side of the fence.

"Don't stick it out at me, you little bastard!" The red-haired boy started towards Jeremy, who darted behind Amos's back. Norman paused. "Get out of the way, four-eyes!"

Amos took his glasses off and put them in his pocket. "I only have two eyes now," he said calmly. The redhead didn't look like a fighter, he thought. He hoped not; he had hardly ever hit another boy, and the idea of tangling with this fat, sweaty one almost made him sick.

He was right. Norman's voice rose mockingly—"Oh, he only has two eyes now!"— but he made no move.

Henry Stiggs, with his pale face and tangled black hair, looked like more of a problem if he chose to be: he was slim, hard, and quick. "Are you going to let *him* scare you?" Henry asked. Then both of their faces grew more serious.

"What happened?" A tall man in khaki overalls was leaning a stepladder against the fence. He wore a short, pointed beard, and horn-rimmed glasses bound to his head by a short leather strap.

"Jeremy got stuck on the fence again, Mr. Cartwright," several voices called. Juliette handed Amos back his jacket. He put his glasses on again.

"Oh, so Jeremy got stuck on the fence!" Mr. Cartwright looked angrily at Jeremy, who had come nearer. "And they called me from the shop to rescue him. Apparently Jeremy can climb down from the fence by himself now, eh?"

"The jungle boy here climbed up and pulled him down," Norman put in. "Like a monkey."

"So you don't have to climb after him, Mr. Cartwright," said Henry Stiggs, keeping a straight face.

The teacher glared at Henry for a moment, then turned on Amos. "Who are you?"

"Amos Okoro."

"Oh, you're the one. I did have some notice of your coming. We locals are always pleased to be made aware of the great world outside."

Norman Glanders whistled; Henry Stiggs snorted. "What *does* bring you here?" asked Mr. Cartwright.

"I came with my mother and father."

"Yes, yes, I understand that. I didn't suppose you'd swum here. And why do they grace us with their presence?"

"They're doctors. They came to work at the big hospital in Kingston."

"We're honoured. And what do your parents, the doctors, have to teach us?"

Amos almost asked this strange man if *he* was a teacher, but decided he'd better not. "I don't think they came here to teach. They came to learn."

"Remarkable!" Mr. Cartwright said. "And at whose feet do they drink wisdom?"

Amos thought back over the names of the doctors his parents had been discussing. "I don't know," he said at last. "I don't know which doctors they'll be working with."

"*Which* doctors? *Witch* doctors! We don't have witch doctors here, young man! Your parents have obviously come to the wrong country!"

Amos shook his head. "I don't mean *dibias*. They came to work with the regular doctors here."

But Mr. Cartwright didn't seem to have heard him. "You must tell us who these witch doctors are. We'd all surely like to know."

He looked past Amos to the door where Mrs. Bidcup had just appeared. Very quickly, he gathered up the ladder and walked back, calling, "Just a false alarm, Vice-Principal."

Amos had been keeping his eye on Norman Glanders and Henry Stiggs. They were now slapping each other on the arm, hooting, "Witch doctors!" But they might not keep themselves amused for long. He looked around for a weapon.

The path along the fence was covered with light gravel and a few largish stones. He had always liked to throw stones. He enjoyed watching their flight as they left his hand, and the feeling that they were still under his control. He would practise against a particular large leaf or branch. In the beginning he'd thrown stones at flying birds too, until he had wounded one and had had to kill it: a beautiful green creature with a long tail. After that he'd never again aimed at anything alive.

The two larger boys were approaching. He checked his thoughts of the village, picked up three stones, and looked for a target.

The bell rang to end recess. The smaller children were now going in; the seesaws were empty. Amos chose the handle of one of them, some thirty yards away, and threw his stones at it rapidly. The first hit the handle sharply; the next two missed it by an inch, and nicked the wood. Behind him, the footsteps stopped. He scooped up some more stones and began throwing at the next seesaw, a little farther away. This time he got three out of five hits. With new stones in his hand, he began to run around the seesaws, aiming at the handles from all angles, hitting them more often than not. He began to prance, in a shaking motion he had once seen during a tribal ceremonial dance on television in his home in Lagos. To his surprise, this made his aim better. Norman Glanders and Henry Stiggs walked towards the school without saying a word.

"That was a good idea," Naomi told him that evening, when he was describing his first day in school. "I hope you didn't mock them, though."

"I didn't say a word to them."

"That's better. Some of these people, you mock them, they just *have* to do something about it. They fancy they have a place in the world to keep up."

"They thought Mom and Dad were *dibias*."

"Did those boys say that?"

"I said something about which doctors my mother and father worked with and this teacher, Mr. Cartwright, thought I meant *witch* doctors."

"Did he really think that?" Naomi sniffed.

"That's what he said. He was mocking me. It made him feel good, I guess."

"What kind of man was he?"

"A thin man. He was light and dried out. But he was afraid of high places."

"Hah!" said Naomi. "Then he better leave those *dibias* alone. *They'd* show him high places!" She chuckled, shaking her head. "Maybe you shouldn't tell your folks about the *dibias*, though."

When Amos came home the next afternoon, he smelled warmth and cinnamon from the kitchen and saw that Naomi had company. She, old Mr. Stern, and Lester Prewitt were sitting around the kitchen table. Just as Amos entered the kitchen, Naomi rose to look into the oven, where a cake was baking. "Your parents want to give a Sunday tea for all the doctors soon and I thought I'd try out this oven with a spice cake. Somehow, I suspected I might have company today."

"I found Mr. Stern taking a walk downtown," Lester Prewitt said, "and remembered your invitation. He didn't seem in a hurry to go home. You remember Amos, don't you, Mr. Stern?"

Mr. Stern reached forward and held Amos's right hand. "Do I remember him? I do remember him. He brought me a duck. Any time you want to bring me such a duck, young man, you should come."

"Well now, we don't want to overdo it," Lester Prewitt said. "Your granddaughter is used to seeing me. I've always been around. She might be suspicious of a new person."

Mr. Stern waved his hand. He looked puzzled, remembering. Suddenly he beamed. "You're Amos! I said bad things to you because of the other Amos, the one who was a prophet."

"I didn't mind," Amos told him.

"But he was a real *mensch*, too," Mr. Stern continued, as if Amos hadn't spoken. "He was supposed to be a simple man, a herdsman. He looked after his goats in the mountains of Tekoah, and he came down to preach at the courts of the kings of Judah and of Israel, to tell them to mend their ways. That's what prophets were supposed to do, and he did it with a voice of thunder."

Here Mr. Stern laughed. "He told them off so well that they told *him* to go be a prophet somewhere else."

"It sounds to me," said Naomi, "like he fancied he'd found the Calabash of Wisdom."

"Now, just what is that Calabash of Wisdom, Miss Naomi?" Lester Prewitt asked. "I heard you say that name once before, but you didn't explain what it meant."

Naomi chuckled warmly. "Well, I will explain it," she told the old fisherman, "as soon as I get something inside this child. This cake should be ready to eat now."

From the pan on top of the stove, she cut a plateful of warm squares of spicy cake which she put on the kitchen table. Amos took his square and a glass of lemonade. He started to get another chair from the living room, but when he heard Naomi begin to tell the story of the Calabash of Wisdom he returned to the kitchen and sat down on a bucket beside the kitchen stove, the warmest place in the room. This was like so many evenings in the village, he remembered, when Naomi and some of the old men—and even Naomi's son, when he could forget that he was a modern man of Nigeria—would sit around in the house, or by the fire outside under the tree, and remember the old tales. Often he had sat up listening until he fell asleep, and Naomi had had to carry him to bed.

"Now, this is a story about Tortoise," Naomi began. She paused, and Amos waited for the hum of laughter that would have followed back home. There, no one had to be told who Tortoise was!

But here they didn't know, of course, and after waiting a few seconds, Naomi added, "We have lots of stories about Tortoise. Some are light and some are dark. He was a tricky creature! You had to watch out for him." She shook her head. "The jokes he played! But sometimes he wasn't as smart as he was supposed to be.

"He had such a reputation for being wise that he decided to collect all the wisdom in the world and keep it for himself. So he got the wisdom of every other animal and put it all inside a big calabash; that's a kind of gourd. Then he was going to store the calabash, with all the wisdom inside it, on top of a tall, tall tree. So he hung that calabash around his neck, down his front, and started to climb the tree. Well, he couldn't do it, no one could. You're a sailor," she told Lester Prewitt. "Could you climb up a ship's mast with a barrel of rum slung on your chest?"

Lester Prewitt laughed.

"Of course not!" said Naomi. "You wouldn't try such a foolish thing. But that Tortoise who thought he was so smart, he didn't know any better. He thought he owned all the wisdom in the world, but he still couldn't climb that tree. But then Hare, *Hare*, mind you, who everyone thought was a very stupid animal, said, 'Why don't you just hang the calabash on your back?'

"Tortoise hadn't thought of that. He tried it and found he could climb the tree with no trouble at all. But long before he reached the top, he climbed down again. And he smashed the Calabash of Wisdom on the ground. Because he said, 'If that stupid Hare has that wisdom, which I didn't gather, then no one can ever own all the wisdom in the world!' "

Lester Prewitt had listened to this story with close attention. "I guess that tortoise was what you'd call a 'smart feller'," he said to Mr. Stern.

Mr. Stern nodded politely, but didn't really seem impressed. "You must have known some really smart people in your time," Naomi told him encouragingly.

"Oh, lots. I knew big professors and doctors. Now I know my granddaughter's husband, the businessman, with his fancy shop. Maybe I'll get a calabash at the market and give it to him." Mr. Stern wrinkled his nose.

"But even smart people can use help," he added. "Sometimes they need a guide. I figured I was pretty smart, but at least I knew when I needed a guide to show me the way through the mountains." He sighed. "The mountains of Tyrol, south of Innsbruck in Austria, on the way to sunny Italy. What a sight! Fir trees! Mountain crags! Valleys! Beautiful! But where to go, how to get through them?"

"Were you running from government soldiers?" Amos asked him, thinking of Naomi and the civil war.

Mr. Stern poked Amos's ribs. "That's what I was doing, *boychik*! Sometimes we called them the laundrymen, because they wanted to turn us into soap. Some of them were already on the main route to Italy, the Brenner Pass. Others were behind, getting the soap kettles ready. But I had a guide, a kind mountain boy who knew the land, and for a little *gelt* and a glass of beer at the other end he showed me the way across. Yes," Mr. Stern reflected, "no matter how smart you are, sometimes you really need a guide."

Lester Prewitt nodded, trying to take this in. "But even if you know the country," he said, "you have to keep moving. Which doesn't always work. When I was with Captain Bogart, we tried to disguise our ship, the *Lake Shark*; we changed its name and colours many times. But we couldn't change its basic lines. There was a Captain Slater of the U.S. Coast Guard, worked out of Alexandria Bay. He had a real nose for spirits, and could think better than we did. If we took the spirits from

Cobourg or Port Jordan, and landed them in Oswego or Rochester or wherever, he'd likely be there waiting for us. If he hadn't been so honest, he would have been a champion bootlegger himself, and a lot richer, too. But often our trick worked: just change your colours and keep moving."

Naomi passed the plate of spice cake around again. "You haven't finished yours," she told Amos. "Take another one to keep it company."

She sat down again, looking critically at the piece of cake in her hand. "Now, this business of moving around is sometimes a good idea. But not always. In my village in our war—do you know about our war?" she asked.

Lester Prewitt looked puzzled. Mr. Stern said, "The war about Biafra?" Naomi nodded. "A civil war," Mr. Stern continued. "You must have had a bad time."

"Very bad. People hated each other. They couldn't trust their neighbours any more. And when the government soldiers came, that was the worst time of all. They were looking for traitors, meaning folk who didn't think the same as they did. And naturally, people were scared when the soldiers came, especially folks you'd call 'intellectuals': schoolteachers, doctors, lawyers, some officials. The government troops didn't trust them at all! There were some trials. You know how the poem goes, the one the mouse told Alice:

"I'll be judge, I'll be jury,"
said cunning old Fury:
"I'll try the whole cause,
and condemn you to death."

When they'd even bother with a trial. So many folks, who weren't really bush people, scattered into the bush. And most of them got away. But some thought it was their duty to go back."

"Like Uncle Joshua?" Amos asked.

"Like Uncle Joshua. That was my husband," Naomi explained. "He knew the government troops would be too interested in the background of the students, so they could figure out which ones would take the wrong side. And the soldiers caught him destroying the school records."

She sighed, and then continued. "But the school superintendent decided he was too old for the bush. Besides, he had a great belief in the power of thought. He decided that if he didn't think about the government troops, they wouldn't notice him. So he dressed up as an old beggar man and sat inside a packing crate behind some piles of vegetables in the market. He just sat there, studying his French irregular verbs and paying no attention to what went on outside. The soldiers were too busy looting the shops to look inside the crate. Then they went away, and he came out, still alive. And everyone respected him for knowing when to be still.... Why are your eyes lighting up?" she asked Amos.

"I was just thinking about the story the stranger told us."

"Do you mean the Yoruba man who came to see his wife's family?"

Amos nodded.

"I remember him," Naomi said. "Which of his many stories do you mean?"

"The one about the man who found a skull in the bush."

Mr. Stern nodded. "A good place for a skull."

"It was lying there, just waiting for him to come along," Amos continued. The doorbell rang. Naomi rose from the table and called, "Come in!" and left the kitchen. In a moment she returned, followed by Mr. Hicks, who was carrying a large plastic shopping bag.

Lester Prewitt rose to greet him. "Do you know Mr. Hicks?" he asked Mr. Stern.

Mr. Stern beamed. "The keeper of the treasure house! I wandered in one day when they weren't looking. They were surprised I went there: where did they think I would go? But I have to be careful, now they know the museum is there. I'll come again some time," he told Mr. Hicks, shaking his hand. Then he sat down at the table again and took another piece of cake.

"So, how's school?" Mr. Hicks asked Amos.

"Fine," Amos said dutifully.

"I saw you there. I can see the schoolyard from one of my windows. You were talking to Horace Cartwright."

Amos nodded. "I guess he was talking more to me. He was mad because I climbed the fence."

Lester Prewitt laughed. "I guess he doesn't like to see anyone else climb."

"Why not?" Amos asked him.

"He was a good carpenter once, with his own business. Then he took a sudden fear of heights and couldn't go up ladders any more. No one blamed him, and people were glad when he got the job teaching shop in the school. But he couldn't admit there was any fault in himself, and it soured his nature."

Amos glanced at Naomi, since he had told her about his run-in with Mr. Cartwright. "My," she said, "you're finding quite a crowd in your school!"

"But I was forgetting," Mr. Hicks said. "I have something for you to read." He took a thick book out of his shopping bag. "This is about the American Civil War, that earthquake we mentioned. And this." He took out a file with a number of sheets of paper stapled together. "It's my article about the bounty hunters—the slave-catchers, as I call them. I finally finished it. You might want to read it when you have time." He looked at his watch. "But I have to go now. Come to the museum and tell me what you think." Then he winked at Amos. "I've kept your artwork—framed it, in fact. My wife loves it! She wants it at home, but I may take it back to the office, if only to see what the colonel says." He picked up his shopping bag, shook Naomi's hand again, refused cake and lemonade, and was gone.

"We'd better be going too," Lester Prewitt said. "They might be looking for you, Mr. Stern. I don't want them to find you here."

"She saw me heading to the library," Mr. Stern answered. "They have a big sale today in the shop. She'll think I'm still among the books. If she finds me there soon she'll think I never budged. As long as I'm sitting quiet and decent by some thick tomes."

"Well, let's go now," Lester Prewitt told him. They left, Mr. Stern pausing to lay his hand on Amos's head.

Amos watched them go down the street, then sat down at the kitchen table again and leafed through the thick book about the American Civil War, which was closely printed and full of tables and maps but no other pictures. A chapter about plantation life and the attempts of slaves to escape looked more interesting but somehow he flipped through the pages without taking many words in.

He looked at Mr. Hicks's article too, and found still more tables in it: columns of figures showing which states the slaves had escaped from, and how many. But one page caught his eye.

"Some of the bounty hunters were ruffians," he read, "avoided by all decent folk. Their sinister aspect betrayed their profession. Others were more plausible: well dressed, soft-spoken, courteous. Some posed as ministers seeking lost members of their 'flocks'. In truth, they were wolves rather than shepherds. One of the dreadful Brimston Brothers had a plump, comfortable aspect that concealed a pitiless, avaricious nature; the other was thin, wraithlike, of a deadly pallor, more like a shadow than a man, but a shadow with a deadly purpose. Their victims thought of them as fiends in human form, demons incarnate."

Naomi coughed. "Are you dreaming over Mr. Hicks's writing? Is it easy to read?"

Amos shook his head.

"That's what I figured," Naomi said. "You'd do better to get him to tell it. I think he'd like that better, too. He strikes me as a man who has more words in him than he knows what to do with. You're lucky he doesn't take himself too seriously."

Amos went back to the article and was trying to read the beginning of it when he heard the car drawing up. His parents came in, his father frowning a little, his mother trying not to laugh. "Well, here's our young artist!" she exclaimed. "We were too busy to notice what you drew on the car. It took Mr. Bidcup himself to find it, when he walked out to the parking lot with us."

"Oh-oh!" Amos groaned.

"Don't worry. He didn't recognize himself. He thought it was some African god. I told him we had only one God, the Good Lord Himself, but he didn't listen. He photographed that dust picture and seemed so pleased! I almost felt I was committing a sacrilege having the car washed."

His father seemed less pleased. "Now, you watch your nonsense. If you want to make fun of people with your pictures, keep it for yourself. You have to remember that we're strangers here."

Naomi shook her head too when they were alone. "You seem to be spreading your artwork all *over* the place. It looks like your sins are catching up with you!"

CHAPTER FIVE

In the Haunted Castle

Amos had thought he might get in trouble for throwing stones, but the only result was that Peter Russell, the captain of one of the baseball teams, invited him to try out as a pitcher. "Chen can catch the ball whenever he pays attention," Peter said, pointing to the Chinese boy in the outfield, who was drawing figures in the dirt with his toe.

But somehow, Amos had trouble with the idea of throwing the ball so that it *couldn't* be hit, and the batters kept knocking the ball into the street. After fifteen minutes Peter Russell said, "Well, I guess *some* of you aren't such good ball players." But he told Amos that he could stay on if he worked on improving his game.

No one else paid him much attention. Even Juliette seemed wrapped up in her own thoughts. Only little Jeremy called to him from the other side of the fence. He had learned to climb down it as well as up, and he often did both. But this didn't please Amos as much as he thought it should.

The air had grown colder: a high-pressure front from the north, someone said. The sky turned a harder blue than Amos had ever known. He wore a windbreaker now, like most of the other students. They didn't seem to mind the cold, but he supposed they were used to it. Henry Stiggs and Norman Glanders watched him with his hands in his pockets, trying not to shiver.

"Say, *Amos*," Henry Stiggs called, "is it cold enough for you?"

"It's all right."

"Not like the jungle, eh?" Henry laughed. "Just wait for the *real* cold weather!" He opened his own windbreaker to show how little the cold affected him. As he walked away, Amos saw that he quickly zipped up again.

Mr. Cartwright's joke about witch doctors had taken on its own life. Entering the classroom one day after recess, Amos saw that someone had drawn on the blackboard a figure with a shield and mask and spear, with the words "Witch Doctor" underneath. He sat down and looked at it, wondering what to do.

When Mrs. Poultney came in, she erased the drawing quickly, shaking her head at the board. "I suppose it's no use asking who did this," she said to the class.

The class looked back at her without a word, except for Juliette, who hissed something under her breath; Amos thought it sounded a little like "Idiots."

"Did you say something, Juliette?" Mrs. Poultney asked. "Do you know who drew that picture?"

"I spoke to myself," Juliette replied. "I don't want to know such people."

The class giggled. Henry Stiggs said, "Ooh la la! The Frog's croaking again!"

Norman Glanders said, "Croak! Croak! Croak!"

Mrs. Poultney rapped on her desk with a ruler, but Henry went on croaking more quietly until Juliette turned to look at him. "*La bêtise, ça pue tellement que ça se trahit toujours,*" she said.

"Now, Juliette," said Mrs. Poultney, "insults don't help. Especially if the insulted person doesn't understand the language."

Juliette shrugged her shoulders and smiled.

Amos liked the next part of class. They were given blank maps of Lake Ontario. Then Mrs. Poultney traced out some of the rivers that ran into the lake on a big map on the wall and had them write in the names. Amos liked to think of the water gathering in all those hundreds of lakes and flowing down the Ganaraska River and the Trent Canal and the Moira River and Salmon River and Napanee River and Cataraqui River to end up in the big lake, on its way to the sea. He could have marked some of the places where the slaves had crossed, too, but decided not to, in case Mrs. Poultney asked him about it. Why should he teach this class *anything?*

Mrs. Poultney collected the maps. "We'd better get on with our social studies," she said. She began to pass some books down each row. "And we have a treat today—*Folktales of French Canada.* I'm sure you'll like them too, Juliette, even though they're in English."

Amos had been watching Juliette's face. She did seem pleased, though her mouth hardly moved. But others in the class were groaning. A few of the boys held their noses. "French!" someone said, then stopped abruptly before Juliette looked at him.

"Be careful with these books," Mrs. Poultney said. "They're on loan from the School Board for a week. We have to give them back in good condition."

"Can we give them back *now?*" Henry Stiggs asked quickly.

"Yes!" several voices called. Norman Glanders snapped his fingers and began to collect the books around him.

"Now, we'll just stop that," Mrs. Poultney said firmly. She frowned. "We were going to read 'The Chasse

Galerie', but I don't know if there's time." She looked at the index. "We have time for 'Fearless Pierre'," she said. "We can read about 'The Chasse Galerie' some other time."

Amos was already leafing through the book, looking for the story. Fearless Pierre! Why, that was the name Mr. Prewitt had given to Pierre Johnson, also a man who didn't know what fear was, except that he avoided the House of the Good Spirits!

Mrs. Poultney began to read. "Once there was a widow who lived on the edge of a forest, working as a cobbler for the village folk. She had only one little boy, who was called Pierre." And she read on. Amos noticed that she didn't read any faster than Miss Nwachukwu, who had taught school in the village—and who had had much the same worried look, he remembered now. He did what he always did in class: read ahead, finished the story, and stored it away in his mind to think of later.

Then he began reading about the Chasse Galerie— about the lumber camp by the Gatineau River in Quebec, amid the deep snow and cold; about the smoky cook-house with the lonely loggers who wanted to go to a dance so far away, and the big canoe that could sail hundreds of kilometres through the air, with the Devil guiding it; you were safe in it as long as you didn't say God's name or touch a cross. But that Devil was no one to fool with! "All that's very fine," Amos read, "but you have to make a promise to the Devil and he's a crea-ture who doesn't put up with a change of heart when you pledge yourself to him." He hoped Pierre Johnson hadn't made any such foolish promise, and then been caught breaking it.

The shuffling and giggling of the class had faded, and Mrs. Poultney's voice. Suddenly Amos realized that they were silent indeed.

"Amos," Mrs. Poultney's voice said. "Amos, I asked you a question."

"Yes, ma'am?" Amos had enough sense to make his question innocent and eager; maybe Mrs. Poultney wouldn't notice that his thoughts had been far away.

But she wasn't so easy to fool. "I can see you've been daydreaming," she said. "Won't you let us in on some of your thoughts?" She tapped on the table to silence the class's giggles with her eyes.

"Well, Amos?"

"I was reading something else. Another story. I finished the one about Pierre."

The class snickered. Even Mrs. Poultney smiled. "You found it too hard to pay attention, I imagine." Then, before Amos could correct her, she told the class, "You must all remember that Amos comes from a different background. Possibly in his country there isn't such pressure to do tasks exactly when they are set out. I imagine his people can look at things from a wider viewpoint. Perhaps they're wiser than we are." Did she really mean this, Amos wondered, or was it something she had been told to say? "But reading is more than skimming, Amos. Just so the class will know you're not getting away with anything, suppose you tell us *your* version of 'Fearless Pierre'."

Amos thought back over the story. Then, before the class's giggles could grow any louder, he said, "It was about a boy named Pierre who was never afraid. One day the King heard that Pierre didn't even know what fear was. So they asked him to spend the night in the old castle, where no one else would stay. Pierre said sure. He asked for some rum, some spirits"—Amos smiled at the word, thinking of Mr. Prewitt—"and some shoes to mend to keep him busy, because he was a cobbler. Then when he was alone at night, some men brought in a coffin with a dead man in it."

Amos stopped to think about the dead man; the class was silent too. "When the dead man spoke to him, Pierre answered right back. When he got sassy, Pierre hit him with a shoe. Then he was sorry and gave him a drink of rum. And the dead man showed him where the gold and silver was buried in the cellar of the old castle. And he told Fearless Pierre that he was the King's father and that he'd been murdered, and he said where his bones were buried in the apple orchard.

"Well, the next morning everyone was surprised to see Fearless Pierre come out of the old castle alive. He told them what had happened and they dug up the bones and buried them properly and said prayers over them; and after that there was no more trouble in the old castle. Oh yes," Amos added, making a face, "Fearless Pierre married the King's sister. I guess he had to. But he was brave. Or was he? Can you really be brave if you're not afraid at all?"

Mrs. Poultney, who had been very still while Amos told the story, didn't answer this question. "Well, you certainly have read the story, Amos. I wonder when. But we've played around enough. I have to give out these assignments for tomorrow."

Mrs. Poultney just had time to hand out some arithmetic problems before the bell rang. She let the rest of the class go, but stopped Amos. "You had read that story before, hadn't you?" she demanded.

"No, ma'am! That was the first time I'd seen it." Amos wondered what he had done wrong. "I just like to read," he explained. "I guess I read too fast."

"Humph," Mrs. Poultney said, shaking her head. "Well, don't be a smart alec. I suppose you know what a smart alec is?"

Amos was going to ask her if it was someone who read too fast, but before he could speak she told him, "You'd better go home now."

He walked slowly out to the yard, wondering what it would be like never to be afraid. The thought of the old haunted castle didn't scare him. That was just a story. The other "Fearless Pierre", Pierre Johnson, must have really been brave! He had had to deal with storms on the lake, and icy water, and enemies with guns who wanted to steal his spirits.

Thinking of guns made him remember what Naomi had said about the government troops. He had heard such talk before, and much worse. In the village the old people, Naomi's cronies, used to talk about the soldiers as if they had been there just yesterday. The government soldiers would shoot you or beat you with iron bars or drag you behind a truck if they didn't like the way you looked, or if you had something they wanted; or if they thought you were disloyal, or for any other reason. Remembering, the old people would shake their heads, and even weep. But, Amos realized, they were proud that they had lived through such bad times. He wished he knew how he himself would act if the government troops were in front of him.

In the schoolyard, several of the students were looking at him strangely. Norman Glanders and Henry Stiggs approached, with serious faces. He looked around to be sure that he had clear space behind him, and to locate a supply of stones, but then judged from the self-satisfied look on both their faces that they thought they could do enough damage with words alone.

"Do you believe all that stuff?" Henry asked.

"What stuff?"

"About the haunted castle?"

"Why not?" Amos didn't, of course, but he didn't feel like denying it to them.

"Would you go in one of those castles?" Norman asked.

"Sure I would."

"I bet!" Henry sneered.

"Now, don't be mean, Henry," Norman said. "Where Amos comes from, they only have huts. How can a hut be haunted?"

Amos thought of some of Naomi's stories but decided not to correct him.

"Yeah," Henry put in. "What was all that about not being afraid? Would you be afraid to go in a haunted house?"

"Maybe not," Amos said.

"I bet!" Henry said again.

"You'd pee in your pants if you saw a ghost!" Norman said.

"I'll tell you when I see one," Amos retorted. "Then we'll see who's scared."

"You'd turn white," Norman said.

"I wouldn't want to." Amos grinned suddenly. "Is that how you got to be *your* colour? Did you see a ghost?"

"Watch it, black boy!" Norman growled. He stepped forward. Amos stooped down for a stone, but Henry took Norman's arm in his long hand.

"Let's have no jungle violence," he sneered. "You just think we wouldn't have any ghosts in a modern city like this. You don't know how close you've been to a real haunted house!"

"Is that so?"

"That's right," Norman put in. "Someone saw you talking to Liquor Lester, by the old Murdoch place."

"What about it?"

"You haven't been inside, have you?" Henry asked.

"Why, is it supposed to be haunted?"

"Sure it is. You wouldn't dare go in."

"It's locked."

"A very good excuse. Of course," Henry added smugly, "you come from a 'different culture'. That means you're more superstitious than we are. You can't help being a coward."

"So" said Amos, "have you been inside?"

Norman Glanders and Henry Stiggs smiled at each other. "We don't trespass," Henry Stiggs said, "especially on Murdoch property. We have to live here, but you're an outsider. There's nothing to stop you, except that you're chicken."

Then the two of them walked off through the students who had gathered around them.

These students remained, many with curious smiles. "You gonna go there, Amos?" a boy called.

"Are *you* gonna go?" another boy asked him.

"I'd be scared!" The first boy laughed. "But Amos won't be scared."

"Why not?"

"Because he's used to spooks already. That's what my dad calls blacks: spooks. He says in some streets in Toronto you can't see anything else."

"And now they're moving in here, too," the second boy declared, walking away.

The others scattered too. Only little Jeremy remained, a finger in his mouth, staring at Amos. But Amos didn't want to talk to him just then.

Amos had seen Juliette in the group too, but now she had withdrawn to the end of the schoolyard. As he walked past her she joined him, her notebook and a stack of library books on one arm. Amos offered to carry some for her, but Juliette shook her head impatiently.

"So you are not afraid to go in that house?" she asked.

"I was just saying that. I wasn't afraid when I was there the first time, but no one had told me it was haunted."

"So now you are afraid?"

Amos took a little while to answer, remembering that this time he was talking to a friend. "I think so."

Juliette nodded. "You cannot be brave if you have no fear." They had come to a long crack in the sidewalk and she skipped along it on one foot, counting the jumps carefully. She stopped, balancing on one foot. "The house *may* be haunted, you know."

"Really? Is that the story around here?"

"Around here? Pooh!" Juliette exclaimed. "Here, they would say anything. But I've watched the house too. No one plays near it, no one goes in. Also, the windows are not broken."

"They're boarded up," Amos told her.

"Not the top ones: a stone could reach them, but no one has thrown stones."

"It belongs to the Murdoch family. They're big people here."

Juliette shrugged. "That wouldn't stop those pigs. Besides, one person did go in: my cousin Henri from Montreal, when he came for a visit. He found a loose shutter on the ground floor."

"Really? What did he see?"

"See? He *saw* nothing." Juliette stopped by a low stone wall and rested her books on it. "There were just some big empty rooms, he said. He thought he heard voices singing up above, a strange old hymn, and maybe even a violin. But that could have been the wind and the trees."

"But he didn't see anything?" Amos demanded.

"No, but something was there, he said. Not in the room with him, but in the next room. Always the next room, or the room he had just left. He went through the whole house, and he was sure there was something there, but always in another room."

Amos whistled. "He sure sounds brave to me! Did he see anything from outside?"

"He thought there was maybe a face in the window on the third floor."

"Where there are no shutters," Amos put in.

"Where there are no shutters. In the window, he said, there might have been a face—but not when he looked right at the window, only just before or just after."

"Was it a white face? A stupid face?"

"I don't know. But he did say," Juliette commented, taking up her books again, "'*Il n'avait pas l'air trop intelligent, celui-là.*' That means, he didn't look too bright."

"Have you ever seen anything around that house?" Amos asked her.

"No. But I was not so interested as Henri. Or you— you are looking at the house now."

It was true; they had been walking along Main Street and each time the house by the lake came into sight, Amos realized, his head had turned towards it.

"It's sure a funny place, that house," he told Juliette. "Do you know, the first time I saw it I almost felt like it wanted me to come in."

"Like you might be welcome there?"

"Yes," Amos agreed. "Maybe too welcome. If I went in, could I get out again?"

He glanced at Juliette, who seemed to be considering his words with more curiosity than fear. "Maybe I will go in," he added.

"Why?" she asked coolly. "To show those *cochons* you're not afraid?"

"No!" Then Amos added, "Well, maybe."

"Don't bother." Juliette kicked at the leaves.

"To show myself I'm not afraid."

"But you are." Then Juliette surprised him. "Perhaps someone in the house needs your help."

"Do you think so?"

"If they take the trouble to call you, there must be a reason. But be careful." She looked at him seriously, then turned down a side street, at a pace that showed she didn't want him to follow.

Amos thought of calling after her, all the same, but what was the use? She was like one of those princesses in the fairy tales: they asked you to do certain tasks without having to explain why. Juliette wouldn't explain, either.

Across Main Street, in the windy alleyway by the museum entrance, Colonel Murdoch was watching Lester Prewitt sweep up the piled leaves. At first the colonel nodded seriously, as if he were in charge. Then the sight of so many leaves going into a large orange plastic bag seemed to sadden him. When some escaped Lester's broom and flew up to the sky he smiled happily. "Look," he told Amos, "some of them can get away. They'll fly out over the lake." He rocked back on the heels of his moccasins.

"And how are you getting on?" he asked, turning somewhat reluctantly back into the street.

"Fine," Amos said dutifully.

"Of course," the colonel said. "Mr. Hicks was sharing his love of the past with you, wasn't he?"

"He sure was!"

"Yes," the colonel agreed, "there *is* a lot of it. But don't let that discourage you. Do you know," he added, stooping down so that Amos would be sure to hear him, "someone once wrote: 'The past is another country; they do things differently there.' Do you think that's so?"

"I don't know." Then Amos shook his head. "How can the past be a place?"

The colonel considered his question very seriously but didn't try to answer it. "Another place, indeed!" he mused, staring at the sky. He no longer seemed to know that Amos was there.

Naomi called to Amos as he entered the house. "Once your homework's done, I'm afraid you have to get all dressed up."

"Why?"

"Because you're invited out to dinner tonight. With Mr. Bidcup and his family. Your mother called. She and your daddy are driving there from the hospital, and you're specially invited."

"Are you coming too?"

"Now, that wasn't made clear," Naomi said, "and I didn't want to ask. I suspect Mr. Bidcup doesn't know what to make of me, any more than your parents do. We'll see. Your mother said you should walk over by yourself, in case they're late. You're to be there by seven. It seems Mr. and Mrs. Bidcup want to learn more about your interest in 'primitive art'."

"Oh, no!"

Naomi winked. "That'll teach you to go drawing your pictures in public places. And on cars, of all things. You'd better think of a story to tell them, so they won't suspect who you were drawing."

Amos thought. "Could it be the beggar who was always cheerful?"

Naomi chuckled. "Yes, that would be a good one. And what if they want you to draw another picture?"

"I don't know," Amos said. "What about Tortoise?"

"Yes, but what story?"

"The Calabash of Wisdom?"

Naomi shook her head. "You'd better keep that one to yourself, with vice-principals and administrative assistants around. You could tell them about the race between the tortoise and the dog, carrying the message to God. Hah, they have a story like that about a tortoise and a hare. If you tell our story, it'll keep them busy comparing for a while. But here"—and she took Amos by the arm—"you sit down with your homework, and I'll get you something to eat before that fancy dinner party."

CHAPTER SIX

The Church of Paul and Silas

Even though the Bidcups' house was only fifteen minutes away, Amos left before six, explaining to Naomi that he had to get a book from the town library. He certainly wasn't in any hurry to get to that dinner party, but he wanted to be by himself first, not to talk to anyone at all.

But just as he got there, the library was closing. People were still reading at the tables and a small line waited at the desk to check out books, but a tall, severe lady stood at the door letting people out one at a time. She shook her head at Amos when he tried the door, then turned her back on him.

He walked down Main Street. The museum lights were out and he didn't even look to see if the street door was open; if there was anyone there, it would only be Colonel Murdoch.

He thought of going back home to wait, but continued down Main Street. In the window of a closed shoe-repair shop a sign in large red letters caught his eye:

LEANDER BLACKMAN
SPIRITUAL DISCOVERIES
CONTACT WITH LOVED ONES
WHO HAVE CROSSED OVER
MESSAGES FROM THE OTHER SIDE
(Seances Thursdays at 8:00 P.M.—Telephone O-SPIRIT)

The sign stirred as if there were a breeze behind it.

A few doors down was Driftwood Fashions, still open but empty. Amos saw a fine red and gold scarf in the window, and stopped to imagine how it would look on his mother's head. As he jingled the few coins in his pocket, a man came to the door from the back of the shop. "What do *you* want?" he demanded. "Where did *you* come from?"

"Be quiet!" a pained voice cried. Mr. Stern's granddaughter walked into view. "Keep your voice down! *Zeyde*'s sleeping at last." She looked at Amos without seeing him. Her husband shut the door.

Amos walked past the shop and down the alley. Mr. Stern was not in the garden; perhaps it was too cool, this late in the day. Soon they wouldn't let the old man out at all, Amos thought.

The sun had set, and the path to the lake was much brighter than the surrounding earth. Amos walked past the old house and on to the wharf, but of course Lester Prewitt wasn't there. His rocking chair was tilted face down on the platform. There was only enough wind to move small waves against the piers with a questioning sound. The lake seemed to be waiting for something.

The old house was black against the sky's last light. Only its top windows shone with light from the lake.

The air was chilly. He had better go home, or else he'd have to go to the Bidcups' early. Then he looked at the back door of the house, which led into a small shed that looked as if it had been built on after the rest of the house was finished.

He certainly hadn't come here to enter the house. But it wouldn't hurt to take shelter in the shed while he waited for old Mr. Prewitt to return.

The one window of the shed was closed by a pair of shutters, but through the crack between them he looked in to a row of empty shelves and another door. The wind was getting colder. Amos touched the padlock, a strong heavy one. But it wasn't really attached to the door frame; it only looked that way from a distance. When he pulled the door, it swung open. He released it quickly and it swung back with a thud.

Amos opened the door again and stepped in. Just inside, by a stack of old boards, was the box Mr. Prewitt stored his carvings in. Leaves had drifted over the box and were piled in a little slope against the inner door that led into the house itself.

Holding his breath, he put his hand on the knob and turned it. The door didn't budge; it must be bolted shut. Only half disappointed, Amos sat down again. He would just wait here with Mr. Prewitt's things; Mr. Prewitt should return soon, and Amos would know his steps when he heard them.

There was still no hurry to go to the Bidcups' house. The clock on the city hall had barely read six as he passed it, and he was sure his parents wouldn't be at the Bidcups' before seven. They had been talking about all the work there was to do the hospital. Even when their shifts were done, they found it valuable to talk to the other doctors or stop by the library—which, unlike the one in Port Jordan, must still be open. If he timed it right, he would get to the Bidcups' just as they did, so he wouldn't have to answer all the questions alone.

Maybe he wouldn't have to tell any stories, either. He began to think of that old one about the race between

Tortoise and Dog. He took out his pencil, picked up a loose board, and drew a picture of Tortoise, with his shell on—because the story must be from the time *after* Tortoise got his shell—and with his head and legs stuck out. This tortoise was really coming out well, the best he'd ever drawn. He looked as if he was ready to walk off the board and away, right into that famous race!

Because the race between Tortoise and Dog wasn't just to see who could run faster. It was life and death for everybody in the whole world.

It happened back in the old days, when people quarrelled with each other all the time. God decided to destroy them all if they couldn't get along better. He told them he'd give them a little time to arrange this, and then—watch out! But they still couldn't agree. Finally, half the people decided to send a message to God, asking that there should be no more Death. And they chose the dog for their messenger. The other half didn't like that solution: they thought Death should come, but take people one at a time. And they sent the tortoise to God with *that* message.

So the two animals set out on the way to God. Of course, Dog was much faster, and he was out of sight in no time. But Tortoise just went plodding along, never stopping. After a while Dog got hungry and went into the bush for food. But Tortoise never stopped; he didn't feel hunger or thirst. He just kept on going. And he got to God first with his message, so ever since then Death has been taking people one at a time.

As Amos looked at the tortoise picture, the shell seemed to grow clearer in the fading light. The lines he had drawn to divide the shell into rounded rectangles became more intense, shining as if they were made of white-hot metal. Their pattern imprinted itself on his eyes and stayed there when he shut them; instead of fading in the darkness as such patterns usually did, it seemed to open out, like a net with holes growing wider and wider, until he felt he could sail right through.

Amos opened his eyes to look at the tortoise again. It was gone! But it couldn't have moved—the board he'd drawn it on was still there. Maybe he'd just knocked the board upside down—but he turned it over and saw that the other side was blank too. Where had the drawing gone?

Then he heard a dry rumbling and rattling, and looked up to see that the tortoise had walked right off its board and was standing by the door of the house! It placed its forelegs on the door and scrabbled forward with its short hind legs until its shell was almost upright. But the door remained closed. Then the tortoise drew back its head and delivered three sharp taps on it with a hard nose.

The door opened slowly outwards. The tortoise scrambled out of the way and lumbered through the opening, the wedge of its shell opening the door still farther. After a moment, the astonished Amos rose to his feet and followed the tortoise inside the house.

The room was very dark, so dark that he looked back in surprise at the shed to see if night had suddenly fallen. No, it was still light enough back there to show the grain of the unpainted wood. Yet when he looked back into the house again, the room seemed even darker than before. He could see no light at all from where the shuttered windows must be.

But where *were* the windows? Shouldn't he have reached the wall by now? His own footsteps as he walked forward, and even the soft scrape and shuffle of the moving tortoise, did not echo as they should have in an ordinary room. He suddenly had the eerie feeling that he was in the middle of a great space.

Then he almost jumped out of his skin, for right in front of him were two pairs of eyes—human eyes.

"Who goes there?" It was a deep voice, full of authority. With the sound, its owner's face became clearer: a black soldier in a long blue uniform and a tall blue hat—like the young man Amos had seen on his first day in Port Jordan, pacing up and down in front of the old fort.

But that had been for the tourists. This was for real. The black soldier moved closer to Amos and the owner of the second pair of eyes—another black soldier, but older—moved forward too. Their buttons glistened in the bright starlight.

Starlight? Amos looked up in astonishment. Yes, it was true: the walls of the house were gone. He was standing outdoors! The lake was still behind him, but the wharf had vanished. There were suddenly a lot of bushes, and two small trees stood to one side, just where the large maples should have been. He looked back along the shore, trying to see the boardwalk and the shops along it. All was dark and empty, except for a few dim lights where Main Street had run a few minutes before. Three lamps hung in the air far away. Could that be the old fort itself?

"Who you got there, Rufus?" the older man asked. "*You*, you keep still. Don't you dare move!" As he spoke, this soldier levelled his rifle and came even closer.

The first soldier, still holding his rifle at a slant, shook his head. "He don't look like any devil, Samuel," he announced.

"You can't be so sure," Samuel said. "They're mighty tricky, these devils and bounty hunters. *You!*" He pointed his gun at Amos. "What's your name?"

"Amos, sir."

"Did that tortoise let you in?"

"Yes, sir. He knew how to open the door."

"Don't call us 'sir'," Rufus said. " 'Sir' is for officers."

He waved to the other soldier to lower his rifle barrel; slowly, Samuel did so.

Amos could hear a faint bumping behind the soldiers as the tortoise pulled itself along. Now that his eyes were more accustomed to the darkness, he could see that they were standing before a tall, narrow wooden building. A church?

"That's a tricky beast, that tortoise," Samuel declared, his hands still firm on his rifle. "Maybe he means some trouble."

"Naw, Samuel," the other soldier declared. "He just shows folks the way here, that's all."

Samuel nodded at Amos. "This one here is different."

"Are you Samuel *Musgrave*?" Amos asked suddenly.

Samuel's jaw dropped. "How'd you know that?" He looked at Rufus suspiciously. "He sure *is* different!"

"And you're Rufus Palfrey!" Amos told the other soldier.

"How do you know our names?" Rufus demanded. But he smiled and set his rifle down.

But Samuel Musgrave and Rufus Palfrey must have died long ago, Amos thought. He wondered why he wasn't afraid. He must be dreaming: soon the soldiers would disappear and he'd be back outside the house. But now they were waiting courteously for him to speak.

"I read what you wrote," Amos told them. "That letter to the commander of the fort." He wondered if he would have to explain about the museum.

He didn't. "Oh Lord, that old petition! Those words Mr. Wedderspoon used!" Rufus laughed, while Samuel grunted in disapproval.

"Is he here too?" Amos asked.

"No indeed!" Rufus said. Samuel snorted. "He went back to England that very year," Rufus continued.

"They said he was 'delicate'," Samuel put in.

"*We* weren't delicate," Rufus said proudly. "We were staying on guard. We're on guard yet."

"They always did stick us with the low duties," Samuel grumbled.

"Don't complain," Rufus told him. "It could always be worse."

Amos broke in. "But what are you guarding?"

"Something that shouldn't be guarded at all!" Samuel snapped suddenly. "What a treasure we do have!"

"Now, Samuel," his companion said, "we're on duty here. You shouldn't question duty when it calls. Besides, our 'treasure' is a close prisoner, much more than Paul and Silas ever were."

"Do you know about Paul and Silas?" Amos asked eagerly.

"Why, sure!" Rufus smiled and pointed over his shoulder. "This is their church."

"Are they *in* the church?" Amos was starting to believe anything was possible here.

"In the church?" Samuel hooted. "They're long dead! And gone above."

"We're long dead too, now that you mention it," Rufus told him. "But we're still down here, and who knows when we'll meet those particular gentlemen? But they did pass on their names to the church."

"Were they bound in jail, all night long?"

"Those were the very ones!" Samuel exclaimed. "The Book says...." And here he set down his rifle, raised his finger, and declaimed:

" 'And the magistrates rent their garments off them and commanded to beat them with rods. And when they had laid many stripes upon them, they cast them into prison, charging the jailor to keep them safely: who, having received such a charge, cast them into the inner prison and made their feet fast in the stocks. But about midnight Paul and Silas were praying and singing hymns unto God, and the prisoners were listening to them; and suddenly there was a great earthquake, so that the foundations of the prison-house were shaken: and immediately all the doors were opened; and every one's bands were loosed.' "

"Oh my!" Samuel sighed. "That was an earthquake!" He seemed to listen for its rumble again.

But Rufus coughed. "We're holding up your visit," he told Amos. "Samuel, you keep watch."

Samuel nodded gravely. He shouldered his rifle and began to walk back and forth before the church's narrow front door, while Rufus walked to the door and knocked solemnly three times.

"Who's there?" a man's voice called.

"Corporal Palfrey. You *know* who I am, you've been watching."

"It don't hurt to ask." But the door was already open. A tall, thin black man peeked out. The moon had risen now and shone on his grey hair, as did the lamplight from the room behind him. "How you doin', Rufus?" he asked.

"Just fine, Strad. We've got us a little business, it seems. We have a real visitor."

"Humph," the tall man said. "Just stand there, boy; let me look at you." He walked back into the church and returned with a lantern. "Did you come from the Big World?" he demanded.

Amos nodded without thinking. But it was true: he had come from far away, across the ocean. Though in entering the old house, he thought, he had come much farther still.

"It figures," Strad said. "Can you go quietly, quietly?" Amos nodded.

"What would you do if you saw a skull in the woods?"

"I wouldn't say a word," Amos assured him.

"You wouldn't! What's that?" Samuel had paused in his patrol and drawn nearer to listen. "If *I* saw a skull, I'd sure say something!"

"You tell him, boy," Strad said. "What's your name, by the way?"

"Amos, sir."

"Amos, like the prophet?"

"I guess so."

"Well, Amos, you tell Samuel why you wouldn't say a word."

"There was this man," Amos said. "He was in the bush, and he found a skull lying there, and he said, 'What is this? How did you get here?' And the skull told him, 'I'm here because I spoke.'"

"Oh my!" Samuel said. "That was a talkative skull!"

Amos continued the story: "So the man ran to the next village to tell the King what he'd found."

"That wasn't such a smart thing to do," muttered Samuel.

Amos went on: "And the King said, 'A talking skull! *This* I have to see!' And he got his court and all his army, and his headsman with the big axe, and they all marched into the bush with the drums beating and the man leading the way. And that old skull was still there.

"But when the man spoke to it," said Amos, "the skull didn't say a word. He talked to it and he yelled at it, getting more worried all the time. And the King's face got harder and harder. And he finally said, 'You called me out here to make fun of me. I'll show you what we do to people who make fun of the King.' And he had the headsman chop the man's head off. They put his body off in the bush and left his head on the ground beside the skull. Then they all marched away, with the drums beating.

"And then, when everyone was gone, that skull *did* speak. It said, 'What's this? How did you get here?' And the head said, 'I'm here because I spoke.'"

Samuel and Rufus shook their heads over the tale, storing it away to consider later. Strad nodded. "Well," said he, "because *you* spoke, because you told the story, you can come in. We had word that someone was coming who could tell stories and help us finish ours. Don't worry: no one's going to chop off *your* head.

"You men wait outside," he added to Rufus, "and keep your eyes peeled. Are the other boundaries guarded now?"

"They sure are!" Rufus answered proudly. "Josiah Stone is by the granite boulder, Jefferson White is down by the graveyard. Samuel, you go mount guard by the old hulk."

They watched him march off. "That's good," Rufus remarked. "Samuel is our steadiest man. Those old enemies really go after that hulk. They expect to find what's gone. But I'm confusing Amos—the boy doesn't understand."

"You're right," Strad said. "You come inside, Amos. All seems to be in order out here."

He motioned Amos through the door and closed it behind him. Now Amos found himself in a tall, plain church with wooden benches facing a wooden altar. On one wall, however, was a fireplace with a couch on either side, and a rocking chair in which a black woman sat knitting.

Half out from the opposite wall was a large television set. It had no dials, so Amos decided they could get only one channel here. Below the screen was written, "Central Office Electronics Co." On the upper part of the screen were golden letters:

SHOW TONIGHT: 9:30 P.M.
PLEASE BE ON TIME.

Amos had just taken this in when he noticed that in the corner nearest the fireplace was a well: a well with a windlass and a dangling rope. A boy about his own age sat on a stump, dangling a fishing pole over the well.

"This is my family," Strad said. "My wife, Martha, and my son, Toby."

Amos bowed to Martha, who smiled sweetly at him. He said "Hi" to Toby, who placed a finger to his lips and nodded. "Are you catching anything?" Amos asked.

"You'll see," Toby whispered. "Some of them are shy to bite. They think they can escape some other way, like we did."

Strad said, "They can only get out if someone fishes them up. *We* were lucky to come straight here."

"What story did you tell when you came in?" Amos asked him.

"We didn't tell a story," Strad replied, "we *are* the story. You can come in and *hear* the story," he added, looking Amos over critically, "but you have a long way to go before you can be part of it."

But Amos persisted. "How *did* you come here? Did you escape?"

"We did indeed," Strad said proudly.

"In a way, we didn't," Martha said.

"Bah," her husband said. "If you're referring to certain physical events, those were only minor inconveniences."

"That's as may be; but there are certain *spiritual* events that are more inconvenient yet."

Toby looked up. "Amos doesn't know what you mean," he pointed out, and then turned his attention back to his fishing pole.

Strad and Martha looked at each other. "What's the matter?" Amos asked.

Finally, Martha spoke. "We can't explain it to you. We have to show you. So's you'll understand. You have to meet Li'l Massa." She bit her lip, frowning. "You'll find it hard," she warned him in a low voice, "but you just have to."

Then Martha closed her eyes, as if she feared opening them again for what would come next. She seemed in such pain that Amos looked away, to her husband. "Why do they call you 'Strad'?" he asked.

Strad smiled. "Now, that I *can* tell you, since Ol' Massa, Li'l Massa's big brother, bragged about it so many times when I was by. He got me in exchange for a violin, an old Eyetalian violin made by a man in Italy called 'Straddlevarious'.."

"That's *Stradivarius*, Pa," Toby said. "Jefferson White heard the name too. He said the man made these violins hundreds of years ago."

"That's right," Strad admitted. "You already told me. But I still like my name for it."

Toby added, "He said those violins are worth a heap of money now."

"Well, I reckon! I guess they're worth *lots* more than I am by this time."

"Don't say that!" Martha had opened her eyes. "You're beyond price. We all are."

"About time, too," her husband commented.

"Listen," said Martha, "we're wasting time. How many nights do you think we have? This boy's folks will be looking for him soon."

"That's so," Strad admitted. "Though we can't rightly tell how time goes here and there."

"And old Mr. Prewitt too, and he's not so easy to fool. He's left us alone so far, but if he thought the boy was in danger he'd come looking for him. Even here. Especially here."

Strad rose from his chair. "Let's go, then." He walked behind the altar, motioning Amos to follow him, and knocked on a door. A peevish voice called, "Come in! Come in! Don't dawdle!"

Strad led Amos into a plain square room that might once have been the minister's office and dressing room. Tattered old black robes hung from nails in the wall. A shelf held a few hymn books with warped covers. On the wall was a map of the Holy Land, showing the kingdoms of Judah and Israel.

But Amos saw all this just out of the corner of his eye. His main attention was drawn to the man who had called out.

He was a large white man, dressed in a dirty white suit and stained vest, sitting on a big wooden armchair. The chair had no cushion, but he had stuffed several black robes under his seat and draped two more over his shoulders. As the door opened he had drawn these robes around him, against the draft.

His face was flabby, spreading towards the bottom, with many pimples showing among the whiskers around his red, moist lips.

Amos thought, he was more frightened when he looked out of the window the first day I saw the old house. But he couldn't have been afraid of me. What scared him so?

The white man wheezed. "Who is this?" he demanded.

"This is Amos, Massa," Strad said politely.

"Has he come to help with the boots? Your Toby can't shine boots properly." Li'l Massa raised both feet from the ground to show his cracked boots, with a hole in each sole.

Amos was going to say that such boots would never take a shine, but Strad's touch on his shoulder silenced him. The white man fell into his own thoughts. "Where's my violin?" he demanded suddenly.

"It's long gone, sir," Strad told him sadly. "But you can make it sing if you like."

Li'l Massa shook his head, looking puzzled. Strad explained, "It was his violin that his brother, Ol' Massa, took and traded for me."

"A rare instrument!" Li'l Massa sighed. " 'Antonius Stradivarius Cremonensis fecit Anno 1711.' That's what the label said. It had a tone like an angel's voice. A fine violinist played it when he stopped for the night with us after a concert in Richmond."

Amos asked, "Did you play it too, sir?"

Li'l Massa glared at him. "Of course I played it. Did my brother send you here to mock me?"

"Your brother?" Amos asked, astonished.

Li'l Massa turned to Strad. "Is that boy trying to ridicule me? Where did he come from?"

"Amos just got here, Massa," Strad said.

"Then get him away again! I can't stand it when they're uppity!"

"When who's uppity?" Amos demanded. Then he felt Strad's hand on his arm holding him firmly.

"Amos is a good boy, Massa," he told the old white man. "He just has to learn."

"Well, you see that he does." Then Li'l Massa shook his head in misery. "Ever since we've come to this place, nothing has gone right."

Suddenly his face was twisted with a terrible fear. Then he relaxed and promptly fell asleep.

Strad put his finger to his lips and tiptoed out of the office, leading Amos by a hand on his shoulder, keeping him quiet with the pressure of his fingers.

Once the door was closed and his shoulder was released, Amos demanded, "Why do you let him talk to you like that?"

Strad smiled. "We're all he has. We're afraid he'll run outside if we cross him."

"Why don't you let him run?" Amos asked. "Then you'd be rid of him."

"You see," Strad explained, "we owe him. We don't want any real harm to come to him."

"What do you owe him?"

"Why, he set us free."

"But he was your *master,* you said so."

They were back at the fireplace again. Strad explained, "He was only the *Little* Massa. That's what we all called him. He was the younger brother of Ol' Massa, who owned us."

Martha shook her head, her eyes brimming. "He's just a poor foolish man who never meant any harm. He talks rough sometimes, but he never actually hit anyone."

"That's right," Strad said. "When Ol' Massa had people whipped, Li'l Massa would run in the house and cover his head with a pillow."

Martha shook her head. "And call out things that made the white folks say he was crazy."

"What things?" Amos asked her.

"He'd call out things like 'Oh, the pity of it!' To me, they made pretty good sense."

"And he played that old violin pretty well," Strad said. "We all liked to listen to him."

"That was real mean of Ol' Massa to take his violin away from him. Still, it did bring Strad to the plantation, or we'd never have met."

"So maybe there was some sense to it after all," Strad agreed. "Besides, sometimes he can still hear that violin."

"Listen!" Toby exclaimed. "There it is now!"

From somewhere up above came the sweet, high sound of a violin playing an old lullaby. "That's it," said Strad. "I know the sound. When he thinks hard enough about the violin, it plays again. I wonder what brought that on. I'll go see, in case he wants something."

He walked into the office, closing the door carefully behind him. In a short time he returned, smiling and shaking his head. "I might have known. He asked me about the new 'piccaninny'; that's you," he told Amos. "You mustn't mind the way he talks, those are the only words he knows. He asked if we'd found you a place to sleep, and if you were warm enough. He said, 'That boy's a stranger. If he's a stranger, he has to be taken in.'"

"Humph," Martha said, smiling. "Sounds like Li'l Massa's getting some religion at last."

"He needs all he can get, with the danger he's in," Strad said seriously.

"In danger?" Amos asked. "*He's* in danger?"

"More than you can imagine! Wait a little, you'll see. Though I wish you didn't have to; I wish none of us did."

"Hey!" Toby called suddenly. "I got one!" He raised his pole, a long one with a line at the end of it, and backed away from the well, raising the pole higher and higher. The line came up with a bottle at the very end, riding inside a circle of hooks like Mr. Prewitt's casting grapple.

"Let's see what you got." Toby's father stepped forward and examined the bottle carefully. "No," he said at last, "this one ain't ready yet. Better toss it back till it's ripe."

"Drat!" Toby said. But he slipped the bottle out of its noose and dropped it back down the well. Amos heard a splash far below. "Not one of them's been ready for days," Toby complained.

Amos asked, "What are they like when they are ready?"

Toby smiled happily. "You should have seen the last one! It played with me before it flew off. You should have seen it zip around in the air! Like a kite, but with no string. It said it would play with me again on the other side."

Martha held up her hand, nodding at Amos. "This boy doesn't understand a word of what you're saying. Do you, child?"

Amos started to shake his head, then stopped. "Are there spirits in the bottles?"

Strad slapped his leg. "That's exactly right! How come you know about spirits in bottles?"

Amos looked down, embarrassed. He thought he had better tell these folk the truth. "Mr. Prewitt told me. But he didn't mean the same kind of spirits."

All the others laughed. "Ol' Mr. Lester!" Strad exclaimed. "He's good company for us. We like to watch him sitting and carving by the lake."

"I like to hear him talk to himself, too," Toby said. "All about his trips on the lake." He was silent, then turned to his father. "Pa, when are we going to make *our* trip?"

Strad touched his son's shoulder. "We have to wait a little."

"We've *been* waiting! When can we go?"

"When the time's right," Martha said firmly. "We're like those spirits in the bottles, we can't get out till we're ready. We're just in a bigger bottle, is all. But I believe we may be ready soon. I feel that last voyage coming."

Her husband and son looked at her in surprise. "I *do* have that feeling," she said. "Also, we're due to have a show tonight. But first, Toby, you show Amos around the place, as far as you can take him. Not outside, this time. And don't bother Li'l Massa more than you can help. He'll need all his strength for the show."

Toby wound up his fishing line and laid the pole over the top of the well. "Come on, Amos," he said.

Amos followed Toby through a side door near the front of the church, and up zigzag stairs to the steeple. They passed a square window as they climbed, and Amos paused to look at the black soldier who was on sentry duty outside, by the lake. Just offshore lay what at first seemed a pile of old timbers; then Amos saw that it was a wrecked wooden sailboat, and realized that it was Samuel Musgrave who, rifle on shoulder, paced back and forth by the lakeshore.

Toby looked over Amos's shoulder. "That's the hulk out there. It brought us here."

"Brought you here? But it's a wreck!"

"Yep, that's how we came to be here. And now the soldiers keep it guarded, at least at night. They rest in the daylight. They get time off when the show's on, too. No one can get near us then."

"But who are they guarding against?" Amos asked.

"You just wait and see! I still don't like to look at them. You won't either."

"*Them?*" Amos asked.

But Toby didn't answer. "Shh," he whispered, "look there!"

It was just a shadow on the water, Amos thought. Then there were two of them. Not solid enough to be men, but too solid for mist, though they walked on the water like pillars of mist—one fat and spreading, one tall and thin.

"Prendergast!" The name came in a whisper, but one that carried far. It could have reached across the big lake, Amos thought; perhaps it had done so.

"Prendergast! Where are you, my dear friend?"

The voice came from the right-hand figure, the thin one.

Now the fat one on the left spoke in its turn. "Does your skin tingle in anticipation, Prendergast? Do you itch? We know how to scratch you!"

In answer, a low wail from below reached the boys in the tower. The fat figure outside chuckled. "Are you aghast, Prendergast?"

"Please!" said the thin one. "None of your vile puns! He doesn't mean it, you know, Mr. Prendergast. It's just his joke. He's lonely for you. He's longing for you. We both are. How can you disappoint us?"

Amos turned mutely to Toby. "They're callin' Li'l Massa," Toby whispered. "His name was Mr. Prendergast."

"But who are they?"

"Don't you know?" Toby stared at him. "Can't you tell? They used to be able to chase us. But now we're free of them. We just have to wait out our time, then we can cross over. Look there!"

By the wrecked hull, Samuel Musgrave had raised his rifle against the two figures who walked so daintily across the water. They were closer now, and Amos could see their faces and their leering red mouths. They were dressed in sober black. The fat one wore a broad black hat, the thin one a shining topper which he held to his head, against the wind from the lake, with a long, pale hand.

"Why, it's old Samuel himself!" the fat one said, and the thin Top-hat added, "How do all the stolen chickens roost in your stomach, Samuel?"

The soldier did not answer, but levelled his rifle at the two figures.

"But I thought they were ghosts," Amos whispered to Toby. "How can he shoot them?"

"He can't," Toby whispered back. "But the rifle gives him courage, and that keeps them away."

"And what about the girls of the garrison town?" Broad-brim asked Samuel. "Remember how you leered at them while you were supposed to be keeping watch? Shall we bring you a few now?"

The sentry held his post, motionless. "Do you remember the marks you put on your wife's face with your fist?" Top-hat asked delicately. Samuel shuddered, but steadied himself again.

"Ha!" Toby whispered. "They won't get old Sam to move by such talk! He knows he wasn't perfect, but he'll do his duty. They can't touch him. They can't pass him, either, and they know it."

"But who are they?" Amos asked again.

"They're the Brimston Brothers. They were slave-catchers once. Now they're something else. They're devils! Devils from Hell!"

"Real ones?" Amos asked. He didn't think he believed in Hell.

"As real as you'll ever see!"

The top-hatted figure called out, "Oh, Mr. Prendergast, Massa, suh! Why do you hide yourself with such low-lifes? Don't you want to meet your true friends?"

A groan sounded from below. "It's *him* they've come for," Toby said. "For Li'l Massa."

CHAPTER SEVEN

The Picture Show

For some time the Brimston Brothers walked on the water, keeping well away from Samuel Musgrave's rifle and calling for Li'l Massa. "Come to the window again," one of them crooned; and the other added, "What a serenade we have for you!"

"A serenade from your very own violin," the first explained, "but now it sings *our* tunes. Don't you want to hear it?"

Li'l Massa didn't answer, but the boys heard him weeping.

"Your new little nigger won't help you," Broad-brim called at last. "You ain't such a fool as to trust him!"

"But really," Top-hat said, growing fainter in the mist, "you should watch the company you keep. Surely you, of all people, aren't becoming a nigger-lover!"

Then both the brothers faded away. Toby watched them keenly. "They won't come back tonight. They can't come in here, so they want Li'l Massa to run out there. Sometimes I think they'll vex him so much that he *will* run, just to get it over with." He shook his head.

"Come on," he told Amos, "I guess we better go back to see the show."

"Will it be on the TV there?"

"Is that what you call it? We wondered. It just turned up the other day. I guess we *are* getting up to date."

"But what did you have before TV?"

"We had our shows, but they were just there. Only there was no writing. 'Course, none of us knew how to read then."

"Who taught you?"

"That's another story. But about this TV: one day, there it was, with one of these crazy announcements. You'll see. Mostly they tell us things we know already."

Amos looked carefully at the television set, which was no more than three feet across. "Say, the shows must have looked pretty funny just out there in the open, without a set around them."

"Well, the screen gets bigger. You'll see. Darn!" Toby had not been able to take his eyes from the well. Now he walked over to it. Amos joined him and looked down. The well was full of deep green water that seemed lighted from below.

"I bet I've seen the show already. I'd rather go fishing again." Toby was unwinding his line from the rod. Just above the casting grapple hung a necklace of bright red beads.

"Is that your bait?" Amos asked him.

"Yeah, but it's only good for ladies. And most of the bottles I've caught with it weren't ready." Toby shook his head. "I was going to tear a page out of one of the prayer books, but old Samuel Musgrave stopped me. Anyway, I'm not sure what it might catch."

Amos felt in his pocket. "What about this?"

"Money?" Toby inspected the quarter with little interest. "No thanks! If they came up for that after all these years they'd be undersized, and likely mean too."

Amos felt something else in his pocket, hesitated, then held out the letter A that Mr. Prewitt had given him. "What about this?"

"Say, now! That's really something! That's brass: did it come from a boat?"

Toby shined the letter on the seat of his pants, then held it up to the light. "We'll sure give it a try!" He glanced at the television set and at his mother, who was nodding to him to come closer. "After the show."

By the fire, Rufus Palfrey, Samuel Musgrave, and two other soldiers had gathered. "This is Josiah Stone and Jefferson White," Rufus said. Amos noticed that the sentries had stacked their long rifles neatly in a corner.

"Howdy," Jefferson said; Josiah nodded. Samuel Musgrave added, "Welcome, young man. May your departure be as happy as your coming." He turned back to rub his hands before the fire.

"Those flames do feel good," said Jefferson White, a short, smiling man who had opened his blue coat to let the heat in. "Sometimes out there I think I'm one of those souls frozen in ice, like Mr. Wedderspoon wrote."

Rufus Palfrey shook his head. "That Mr. Wedderspoon did have a way with words."

Josiah Stone, a silent, solid man with huge shoulders, held up his hand but thought long before he spoke. "Them were *his* words. Why do *we* have to be stuck with them?"

"Now then, Josiah," Samuel Musgrave reproved him. "The Lord does work in mysterious ways."

"Humph," Josiah growled.

Jefferson White slapped his hands together. "It was all those words he wrote about Purgatory that did it. 'Now we ask, to what place have we been sent? Have we come from Hell to Purgatory?' Seems like the higher authorities were taken with that line and decided to let us go on as we had started."

"But what *is* Purgatory?" Amos asked. He had heard the word before, he thought, but didn't know its exact meaning.

"Well now, we had lots of discussion on that," Rufus Palfrey put in, just before Samuel Musgrave, who was drawing a long breath, could speak. "We figure it's a kind of halfway place between our old world and the next one."

"It's where we come to atone for our sins," Samuel said sternly.

"Well, we do that too. But mainly I think it's where we have to wait till the folks in charge figure we're ready for them; or they're ready for us. Anyways, it could be worse."

"It could indeed," said Samuel Musgrave. "Why, we might be like those poor spirits in bottles, ripening away down at the bottom of the lake—like the ones Toby fishes up."

A new light shone on the fireplace. The TV screen had begun blinking on and off. "The show's going to start in a few minutes," Toby called. The soldiers left the fire and began to set up seats for the show. They pulled two of the long benches around so that they faced the screen. Two of them fetched Martha's armchair and placed it between the benches. They stood behind the benches to get a little more warmth from the fire, still talking about Mr. Wedderspoon.

"But tell me," Josiah Stone asked everyone and no one, "how come we got to do our Purgatory here and he don't?"

"Now then, Josiah, it surely ain't all comfort and ease for him back in England," Jefferson White assured him. "You remember how he was always talking about that old church of his back home? Likely he's a mouse there now, living off crumbs from the altar."

Rufus Palfrey laughed. "You remember those long sermons he used to preach? I bet he has to listen to them himself now." He slapped his leg. "*I* tell you what: he was turned into one of those wooden church statues he was always talking about, and he's stuck there, hearing all the other preachers go on!"

All the soldiers laughed, except Samuel Musgrave, who shook his head. "Now, don't be so hard on poor Mr. Wedderspoon. He did the best he could; and he was a kind man, too."

"That's so," several voices replied.

A door opened. Strad came in, followed by Li'l Massa. Martha and Toby at once got to their feet. Toby poked Amos and he rose too, unwillingly. The soldiers stopped talking but remained seated.

Li'l Massa looked at the row of black faces and shook his head sadly. "*This* is my punishment." He sat down in the armchair with a look of despair.

"No, sir," Strad told him respectfully but firmly, "*this* is not your punishment."

"Shh!" Toby whispered. "Now the show is really going to start!"

The light in the church dimmed. Amos looked up into the roof-beams, but saw no light bulbs. The oil lamp on the kitchen table seemed brighter, until Martha turned it down. From somewhere above them a solo violin sounded, and then the music of a full orchestra flooded down into the old church. On the TV screen words appeared:

A JOURNEY'S BEGINNING
AND ITS SURPRISING CONTINUATION

Then the bounds of the screen spread, so that it filled all the space before them like a wide stage. The words on the screen, gold in a silver band, rose and spread out like a banner in an arc above the stage.

But now Amos had eyes only for the figures that appeared before him. They were so clear and three-dimensional that he'd have been sure he was watching real people, except that one of them, Strad, was sitting right beside him. Strad was resting his hand on Li'l Massa's arm, as if to prevent him from rising.

But there was another Strad in the space in front of them. Strad dressed in a beautiful black long-tailed coat and top hat, beside an open carriage harnessed to two fine horses. "That's just how I was," the Strad beside him whispered in Amos's ear. "Dressed like a dandy, and sometimes proud of it, too, like a poor fool."

"Shh," Martha whispered. "Ol' Massa's comin'."

The man who stood before them now was clearly Li'l Massa's brother. An older brother: a hard man, despite his girth. A man sure of himself and of his possessions.

"Are the horses ready, Strad?" Ol' Massa asked.

"Yes, Massa," the Strad on the screen said, with a humble tone in his voice that Amos had not heard before.

"Is Mr. Leander's trunk packed?"

"Oh, yassuh." Strad nodded at the back platform of the carriage, which held a wicker hamper and a large black trunk. "It's all ready."

Ol' Massa sneered. "I suppose he put in his books of poetry?"

"Yassuh, he's got *plenty* o' books," Strad said, "an' his clothes, too."

"That should last him. Now, you will spend the night at Mr. Purvis's house in Liberty. He's expecting you. He has a room for my brother."

"Yassuh."

"You are to sleep by Mr. Leander's door," Ol' Massa continued. "Ask Mr. Purvis for a straw pallet; tell him I want you to sleep there, so that my brother does not wander out at night. And the next morning, as soon as may be, you are to be on the road to Prosperity. You should arrive in the afternoon, provided the bridge over the Liberty River has been repaired. But if you must put up at an inn on the way, Mr. Leander has money in his inside pocket. He will count out the proper amount. Again, sleep outside his door."

"Yassuh."

Ol' Massa frowned and fingered his lips. "In any case, in Prosperity you will ask for the house of Dr. Carver. He too is expecting you. If he should be absent, you are to stay with my brother until the doctor arrives. Say nothing at all to disturb him. When Dr. Carver instructs you, you will return here with whatever messages he chooses to send, written or oral."

Ol' Massa pulled at his chin. "Another thing: Mr. Leander is to eat well during the journey. You have a picnic basket for him, I believe."

"Oh, yassuh!" Strad said. "My Martha packed it *real* good. It's back there in the carriage, in the hamper."

"*Your* Martha?" Ol' Massa said scornfully. "Humph. Anyway, see to it that he eats at Mr. Purvis's as well. You are to wait on him at table, as his personal body servant. I believe you have some influence on him."

"Li'l Massa is so kind to me."

"Yes," Ol' Massa snapped. "He would be. To continue: keep him well fed. Plenty of food makes him docile. Do you understand all that?"

"Oh, yassuh, I surely do."

"Well," Ol' Massa grumbled, "at least you have some grains of sense in you; you're not scatterbrained like the rest of my niggers. But don't let that go to your head. I've still got my eye on you."

"Oh, yassuh! I *knows* you have."

Ol' Massa looked carefully at Strad's fine clothes. "I see we've got you well fitted out. I'll wager you never expected such clothes when you were a field hand."

"Oh, no, suh! These is fine!"

A feeble cough sounded in Amos's ear. "He did dress you up well, didn't he? Do you recall those days now?" Li'l Massa wheezed to the real Strad, who only grunted in reply.

"Shh, sir." Martha spoke softly. "We mustn't interrupt the show."

Li'l Massa nodded. "That's right. We mustn't interrupt the show." He settled back to watch.

They saw Ol' Massa walk away, to return shortly holding the arm of his younger brother. Li'l Massa was dressed just as he was now, except that his white clothes were spotless and his boots were whole and shiny.

"Here is Strad to drive you to see Dr. Carver, Leander," Ol' Massa said.

"I know who Strad is," Li'l Massa replied testily.

"Of course you do," his brother said. "He is to look after all your comfort. You can count on him."

"What you mean, brother, is that *you* can count on him. You can count on him to lead me to my keepers."

Ol' Massa closed his eyes patiently. "Don't talk that way, brother. You know how sorry you'll be afterwards."

Li'l Massa turned his head like a turtle's in its shell. "Where are the chains?" he demanded. "Where are the guards?"

Ol' Massa looked even more long-suffering than before. "There are certainly no chains and no guards. I just think you would be more comfortable with Dr. Carver while your room is being repainted."

"It has been repainted," Li'l Massa insisted. "To *my* taste."

"You went a little beyond your bounds there," his brother observed drily. "You may fancy you can daub sunsets and swamps on the walls of the room you occupy, but in *my* house we keep art in its place. The room will be repainted again. But of course, you are the best judge of where you should go—we could always tidy up one of the nigger shacks for you. You do seem to enjoy their company. Is that what you'd prefer?"

Li'l Massa's face slumped. "Have it your own way," he said at last. "I know you will in any case."

Then the audience saw him climb into the carriage behind Strad. His older brother carefully spread a rug over his knees, as if to close him in.

"Where are we going?" he asked in a resigned voice.

"Your driver has his instructions," Ol' Massa replied. "But here are the addresses, in case he has any questions." He put a slip of paper into his brother's breast pocket.

As the carriage drove off, the scene swung to a view of a grand plantation house with six tall white pillars and a long drive shaded by a double row of graceful oak trees.

In the audience, Strad spoke. "Ol' Massa was a mean man. He wanted that Dr. Carver to keep his brother locked up and never let him out."

"We all knew that," Martha replied mildly, "but now they're coming to the meeting place. This is the part I really like."

The carriage had entered a deep forest and shadows covered the faces of driver and passenger. In a short while Strad drew on the reins.

"Why are we stopping?" his passenger demanded. "Are you waiting for the guards?"

"No indeed, suh. But you is all dusty." Here Strad produced a small whisk-broom and brushed off the front of Li'l Massa's coat. As Li'l Massa, evidently used to this kind of service, raised his chin, Strad dexterously slipped the piece of paper from his pocket and made it disappear up his sleeve.

"There," he said, "you is all neat again, Massa. Besides, we is waiting here for the rest of your *en*tourage. And here they is!"

A sound of footsteps on leaves, and then Toby and Martha stepped into the picture. Toby wore a small tailcoat like his father's. Martha, all smiles, was dressed in sober blue with a wide blue bandanna around her head and a large picnic basket on her arm.

"I bet you was wondering what you was goin' to eat, Massa," she said cheerily. "Or who'd look after your clothes and boots. Well, we're all here now."

Li'l Massa shook his head, very puzzled. "My brother said nothing about your coming."

"He jus' didn't want to bother you, suh," Strad said, very respectfully. "But he surely didn't want you to make such a trip with only me to look after you. *That* wouldn't be fittin'! Come on, you two!" he called briskly to his wife and son. "Git on up here! You're keepin' the gentleman waitin'."

Martha quickly stowed the picnic basket in the hamper behind the carriage and climbed up to sit on the hamper. Toby took his seat beside his father. Strad cracked his whip and the carriage set off again into the distance.

The lights on the scene faded, and came up again on a stop for a picnic lunch. Martha laid a fine groundcloth and fetched cushions for Li'l Massa's seat. Strad poured his wine—a good deal of wine—and carved the chicken, while Toby looked after the horses and cleaned up afterwards. Finally Li'l Massa climbed back into the carriage, heavy and content, and fell asleep.

In the next scene, dusk was falling as they drew up by a deserted barn amid a grove of trees. "We is almost in Liberty, Massa," Strad announced happily. "Martha and Toby is going to get supplies at this farm and find a place for the night."

Li'l Massa looked around suspiciously. "But we are going to the house of Mr....of Mr...." He fumbled for the piece of paper his brother had put in his pocket, didn't find it, and looked to Strad for guidance.

"*We* is going to Mr. Purvis, Massa. These two is to stay with his niggers, but I'm to go with you and look after you."

Li'l Massa nodded and closed his eyes again. Strad looked up and down the road and motioned the others to get down. They walked quickly into the barn, and the carriage drove on.

"Oh, Lord!" the real Martha said, "I do remember that barn. It rained up a storm that night, and the roof leaked so there was hardly a dry corner, but we knew we had to stay there, and we did."

"Look at what's happening now," Toby told her.

The carriage with Li'l Massa and Strad had arrived at a two-storey wooden house with wide verandas. The noise of the wheels on the gravel drive brought a small, moustached man to the door, and he stepped forward coldly to shake Li'l Massa's hand. "Come in, Mr. Prendergast," he said, "we've been expecting you.

"You, boy," he added to Strad. "Take that carriage around the back. My boy Pompey will show you where to put up the carriage and the horses."

"Yassuh," Strad said.

Li'l Massa, still half asleep, looked around him, dazed. "Where are the other niggers, the cook and the boy for my boots?" he asked.

Mr. Purvis looked suspicious. He drew a letter from his coat pocket. "There's no mention of anyone but your driver."

Li'l Massa shook his head, as if to clear his ears. "My cook, and the boy for the boots," he repeated.

Strad stepped quickly to his side. "They'll be along d'rectly, Massa," he said softly. Then he turned to Mr.

Purvis. "He's jus' a little confused, suh," he whispered. "I'm the only one with him."

Mr. Purvis accepted his statement without question. "Well, I told your master I'd put his crazy brother up for one night. And of course he needs a driver, or"—he chuckled—"he'd go wandering off in the sky, from what I hear. But I sure didn't count on any other niggers."

"Oh, nossuh," Strad told him. "They's jus' me."

Mr. Purvis turned to look at Li'l Massa, who had sat down on a stone bench beside the carriage and had closed his eyes again. "Well, get the horses to the stable," he told Strad. He touched Li'l Massa's arm. "Wake up there, Mr. Prendergast! I'll show you to your room."

The next scene showed the carriage leaving Liberty, very early the following morning. Soon it stopped by high grass in a sheltered road and Martha and Toby took their places, hardly noticed by Li'l Massa, who was sunk in sleep and misery.

"We mus' make haste now," Strad said, cracking his whip. "Or else that river will be too high to pass." The carriage sprang forward, rattling, so that Martha had to hold on. Soon they were driving alongside a wide stream, swift with foamy rapids. "That's Liberty River," Strad said with satisfaction to Toby beside him on the wagon seat. "And it's right high." The carriage sped along to a wooden bridge whose bottom timbers were already washed by the rising waters. Strad stopped the carriage by the bank, got down, stepped on the bridge, and looked keenly upstream.

"What's happening now?" Li'l Massa's querulous voice sounded above the rushing water.

"Oh, Massa," Strad told him, "I don't think this bridge is safe for us to cross. We better wait a bit till that bad water goes down."

Li'l Massa leaned forward with half a show of interest. "*I'm* in no hurry to enter my prison. Go back, by all means."

They returned by the same road at first, but then Strad took a side road and drove through small, winding forest tracks until they came to a crossroads hamlet of three shacks and a low tavern. On the tavern steps two white men sat, one whittling a branch, the other spitting in the dust. "Gennulmen," Strad moaned, "I is lost."

"Whar you goin', nigger?" the whittler asked, barely looking up.

"I don' rightly know, suh," Strad whined. "My massa was to cross the bridge over Liberty River but the water is so high and so fierce that I'm plumb skeered we'll be drownded if we try it."

"Do we stop here?" Li'l Massa demanded. "Here?" He looked around in disgust.

"No, massa," Strad told him. "I'm jus' tryin to get d'rections from these gennulmens to a *hotel*, where you can rest till that water goes down."

The spitter spat over the carriage wheels. "Do you know a hotel, Jud?"

The whittler shaved down his branch to a fine point. "A *hotel?* Widder Sankey has a boardin' house down towards Liberty way. Don't rightly know whar it is, though."

"Oh, a boardin' house will be jus' fine, suh," Strad said gratefully. "We'll go right along dah. And much oblige', gennulmens, fo' yo' kineness."

The spitter aimed at the right horse's rear hoofs, and addressed Li'l Massa. "Say, mister, where you all headed for now?"

Li'l Massa stared at him. "To prison, to prison," he said.

Strad gave a shrill laugh, startling the horses. "No suh! That's jus' your joke, suh! That's jus' his joke, gennulmens. We is on the way to Prosperity, and that's *exactly* where we'll go when the waters of that creek go down. Thank you *so* much, gennulmens."

He wheeled the carriage around, went along at a leisurely trot until the crossroads was out of sight, then swung off to a side road. "I just hope I remember the way back," he muttered to himself. Sure enough, in a few minutes the carriage was back at the bridge.

They were none too soon. As the carriage approached the river, the water had risen over the bridge's planks. The horses balked at the racing stream but Strad took off his top hat, cracked his whip, and yelled, "Giddap thah!" and the horses drew the carriage across the bridge, its wheels throwing up walls of water on either side.

Once across, Strad halted the carriage and looked back at the bridge. He waited. In another few minutes the river had risen higher and had washed away a portion of the handrail. "I bet the whole bridge will go," Strad said to himself, "but I won't stay to watch."

"Yes, that's what I did," the real Strad said to Amos. "I crossed the bridge at the last second, just before it was washed away. But first I left word behind that I *wouldn't* cross it. See, that's why you saw me talking to those dumb white folk back at the crossroads. That was a place where nothing ever happened. Just to see a carriage like ours, with a dandy black driver, *and* a cook, *and* a boot boy, *and* a big white man besides, in a white coat—why, they'd talk about that for days. And that's what they must have done. I knew that when someone came along to ask, they'd say we were on their side of the creek when we were really on the other and long gone.

"But next I had to talk to Li'l Massa; look at the picture show."

In the show Li'l Massa was now quite awake. "Where are we?"

"Why, we jus' crossed the river, Massa," Strad exclaimed jubilantly. "Now there's no turnin' back!"

He touched the horses gently and waited until they had driven out of sight of the river, then stopped and faced Li'l Massa. "Of course, I don't want to go against your wishes, Massa; but I did have the feelin' you wasn't exactly eager to get to that Dr. Carver's house."

Strad smiled very sweetly at Li'l Massa, who had pulled his blanket around himself without answering. "What do you mean?" Li'l Massa croaked at last.

"Well, Massa," said Strad, "it ain't for me to say; but if you're not pleased with goin' to one place, I wonder why you wouldn't go to another one."

"Another one?" Li'l Massa mumbled.

"I mean, you're a gentleman of leisure now; you could jus' travel aroun' a bit, with us to look after you real good."

"But we're supposed to go to Dr. Carver's," Li'l Massa said weakly.

"Well, yes," Strad conceded, "but we don't necessarily have to go right away. Ol' Massa didn't say that."

"Didn't he?"

"No suh. He said we could get there when we could. Like if the river was so high we couldn't cross over the bridge. Well, you saw, it sure *is* too high to cross now. So you might have a lot of time to do yo' travellin'." While he spoke, Strad started the carriage up again and increased its pace.

Li'l Massa looked back at the road. "He'll follow after us and catch me."

Strad nodded. "Well now, Massa, Ol' Massa *might* do that. And of course, with you dressed like *you* is, and we dressed like *we* is, we'd be pretty easy to know. So maybe we'll jus' play a little trick."

"A trick?"

"Well, we might just change clothes from time to time. Let us show you." Strad drew the carriage up and nodded to Martha, who got off the hamper, opened it, and drew out two long blue coats and broad black hats. She handed one coat and hat to Strad, who quickly changed from his frock coat and top hat, while she put on the other coat over her dress, pulling the hat well over her hair. Then she put Strad's clothes into the hamper but held it open, and in an instant Toby had climbed in. Martha closed the hamper and joined Strad on the driver's seat.

Li'l Massa had watched all this, open-mouthed.

"So you see, Massa, before we was a man and a woman and a boy, dressed fancy. Now we is two men dressed plain. If someone was lookin' for us, he might not know us now."

Li'l Massa managed to close his mouth. Then he said, "But *my* clothes...."

"Well, you're right, Massa, that pretty white suit of yours does stan' out. But Ol' Massa was kind enough to give you some other clothes too; they're in your trunk."

"So Massa, if you likes," Martha put in, "we can *really* go see the world." Li'l Massa could only stare at her.

"Course, if you say so, suh, I can prob'ly find our way to that Dr. Carver's house. If you don't want to roam no mo'." Strad turned to look at the white man with a faint, encouraging smile.

Li'l Massa's face broke into a happy grin. "No! Let's go see the world!"

Strad laughed happily in turn and cracked the whip. "Yes *suh!*"

As the carriage headed down the dusty road, the lid of the hamper rose and Toby's bright eyes shone out.

CHAPTER EIGHT

Escape from an Imperfect World

The images in front of the audience darkened, then disappeared. The glowing boundaries contracted until, as the lights in the church went up, there was again a large television set before them, with the word "INTERMISSION" in gold letters on the top of the screen. The soldiers rose and stretched, then stood around the fire. Strad accompanied Li'l Massa to his own room and shortly returned.

"I just love that part where you fool all the white folks," Jefferson White told him. "I never get tired of looking at it."

Strad smiled modestly. "That was something I learned early. Just talk more ignorant than they did and let them think they were the ones who were deciding."

"Only those words up there get in the way of the story," Jefferson added. "Besides, we know all that already."

"I sure do!" Toby exclaimed. "I'll just skip the next part. I'd rather go fishing. I want to try out my new bait."

"We can still learn from the shows," Samuel Musgrave called to him, but Toby was on the way to the well.

"Amos hasn't seen the show before," Martha told her son, who was already lowering his hooks. "I think the words were there for him. It wouldn't hurt for you to see it again." But Toby just shook his head and concentrated on his fishing.

"Are all the shows like this?" Amos asked Martha. "About what happened to you?"

"That's right. And about what we once were." Martha lowered her voice. "Poor Samuel Musgrave had a wife and family back in Virginia. Then in that 1812 war, when the English sailors landed, they said they'd set him free in Canada if he'd serve as a soldier there. If he'd stayed, he'd have been sold anyway. But he still blames himself for leaving his family, even if he sometimes beat them because life vexed him so. Some of the shows made him remember how he treated them. At first he didn't care; then he started to cry when he saw what he had done, and the other soldiers cried with him.

"Now, Jefferson White never had a wife. He was a real good carpenter; sometimes he even talks about repairing that old wreck of a boat out there. His master hired him out all over the country, and he thinks maybe he has some children here and there. Still, it was easy for him to cut and run.

"And Josiah there, he had to leave his old mother, but she made him go. He's not worried: he knows he'll meet her on the other side, when we finally get there."

Martha was silent for a while, thinking. "What about Rufus?" Amos asked her.

"Well, Rufus had lots to unlearn. He had been a driver before: a black driver of black men." She nodded at the screen. "I don't know how many times we've seen him there, out in the fields or on the riverbank, keeping the men moving along, pulling weeds and loading boats. He wore a wide hat and he cracked a big black whip. Seems like he *enjoyed* using that whip and being a boss.

"It turned out he was a good boss even without a whip; that's why they made him a corporal at the fort. But the show taught him what he'd once been. He's gone through all that, now."

The lights in the room flashed three times, waited until Strad brought Li'l Massa in, then darkened. The screen spread as before, and the words appeared:

THE GREAT ESCAPE CONTINUES

A series of short scenes followed. The carriage was seen travelling through different small towns, fields, and forests, by night and by day. Sometimes the carriage had Strad and Martha as drivers, sometimes only Strad. Li'l Massa was dressed in a white suit, in a black suit, in a checked suit, in overalls with a straw hat and looking decidedly ill at ease. Strad did most of the talking, asking for help for his "pore sick Massa" from sympathetic ladies, ministers of the church, and upright citizens.

Now new words appeared:

INTO PARTIAL FREEDOM:
ON THE BORDER BETWEEN MARYLAND,
A SLAVE STATE,
AND PENNSYLVANIA, A FREE STATE

The next scene showed the outskirts of a village in the hills. The carriage was drawn up by a fork in the road, near a grove of trees already touched by autumn. Just down one branch of the road was a bridge over a quiet river; the other branch continued along the river. Li'l Massa sat in the carriage, with Strad and Martha standing nearby. Toby entered, walking along the road

with a fishing rod over his shoulder, a few steps ahead
of a small, sharp-eyed, red-nosed man with a shotgun in
his hand. Toby whispered to his father, sauntered to the
stream, and dropped the bait in.

Strad walked to the carriage, straightened Li'l
Massa's tie, and dusted off his smart grey coat. "Now,
you be sure to ast him where we at, Massa, *please*," he
said in a low but pleading voice. "I *thinks* we is going to
cross into Delaware, but I can't be sure." He drew back
as the stranger came closer.

"Evenin', sir." The stranger nodded respectfully to
Li'l Massa.

"Good evening," Li'l Massa replied with dignity.
"Does this road lead to Delaware?"

"Delaware!" the man hooted. His red nose seemed to
glow with joy. "Mister, are you ever lost! Who told you
this was Delaware?"

"My nigger driver did." Li'l Massa nodded to Strad,
who stood by the wagon, hardly daring to raise his eyes.

"Your nigger! Well, no wonder you're lost if you
depended on *him* to guide you, friend."

The red-nosed man cast a keen look at Strad, who let
his eyes fall modestly and shuffled his feet.

"Imagine," the red-nosed man continued, "trustin' a
slew-footed slack-boned nigger to show you the way.
You're lookin' for Delaware, my friend? Well, you're
heading right for Pennsylvania!"

"Pennsylvania?" Li'l Massa mumbled in disbelief.

"Yes, sir! You went *prezackly* the wrong way. Fact is,"
the red-nosed man added confidentially, "when I saw
that there black crew of yourn I wanted to have a little
closer look. That's Yankee territory across there. Not
far down the road there's a farm with those folk they
call 'Friends'. Some friends! Friends of the Divil, I'd
say. They're those Quakers, and ever' one of 'em is a
low-down Abolitionist!"

He nodded at the bridge. "The word's got around, too. Some of these niggers come here bold as brass, thinkin' they can just walk across to the promis' land, where they'll never have to work again. Well, I make 'em think different." He tapped his shotgun barrel. "I've made a fair business catchin' a few. Why, for a buck like yours, with a market value of a thousand dollars, I'd get a hundred when the goods is delivered back to the rightful owner. Saves the trouble of crossin' over to bring 'em back, which I have every right to do, now that the laws are on our side."

Li'l Massa regarded him, open-mouthed; so did Strad and his wife. "*That's* the road you take, my friend," the red-nosed man continued. "You just head due east, but you ask whenever you come to a fork in the road. That way you'll get to Delaware in God's good time." He looked across the river and snickered. "To Delaware, not Pennsylvania."

Strad approached the two white men very timidly. "Massa, doesn't you wan' to eat now? They's a table under that tree, right handy."

Li'l Massa smiled happily.

"An' this gennelmun too, who's been so kine. Does he wan' to eat somethin'?"

"Well, I don't mind if I do," the red-nosed man announced before Li'l Massa could reply. The stranger looked approvingly at the basket on Martha's arm. "I bet your Mammy there's a fair cook," he told Li'l Massa. "It often happens that if they don't have brains in their heads they'll have 'em in their fingers."

Martha beamed. "Oh, *thank* you, suh!"

The scene continued with Li'l Massa and the red-nosed man sitting at a wooden table near the road, being served lavishly by Martha, with Strad acting as generous wine steward. A few loafers came to watch but at the red-nosed man's frown they withdrew, licking their lips.

Li'l Massa grew sleepy and turned his glass down, but the red-nosed man kept asking for more, which Strad willingly supplied, soon switching from wine to whisky. He eyed the level in the bottle uneasily; it was almost empty before the red-nosed man suddenly became unconscious, with his eyes wide open. Strad waved a hand before the man's eyes. No response. He signalled to Martha to gather up the cloth and basket. Very carefully, he unloaded the shotgun and tossed the shells into the river. He conducted the sleeping Li'l Massa to the carriage and gently, whispering to the horses to be quiet, led the wagon into the trees that shielded them from the village. He had to throw a pebble to draw Toby's attention away from the stream. Toby came running with his fishing rod and quickly jumped aboard the carriage, and they rolled across the bridge into Pennsylvania.

Strad, at Amos's side, spoke thoughtfully. "That sure was a suspicious man. I could tell from his eyes that he still had some questions to ask. But his nose showed me what he *really* liked." He shook his head. "My, I didn't think we'd have enough liquor to fill him up. We had to go right to the bottom of the bottle."

The next scene was announced with these words:

IN PENNSYLVANIA, A STATION ON THE UNDERGROUND RAILWAY PROVES TO BE ONLY A QUICK STOP

They saw a farmhouse kitchen, Strad and his family seated at the table. A white woman had just come through an inner door to join them. Her eyes were dark and watchful, her voice discreet. "Mr. Prendergast is still sleeping," she said. "I thought it best to let him get his rest."

Strad and Martha smiled in relief. Toby whistled and drummed his fingers on the table. "I spoke to him earlier," the woman continued. "If I may ask thee: is he quite right in his head?"

"No, ma'am!" Toby said proudly. "His brains is all scattered!" He turned his finger rapidly alongside his head.

"You stop that, boy!" Strad told him. He turned to the white woman. "There's a lot of good things in that head of his, Miz Eliza, even if he gets confused at times. His mind's full of poems and such. When he forgets that he's supposed to be the master and we're supposed to be the slaves, he can be right good company."

"That's right," Martha added. "I thought he was too good for the other white folk on the plantation. Of course, I never said *that*."

"Thee was wise. But why is he still with you?"

Strad hesitated. "We know we'd travel better without him. But we just couldn't bring ourselves to leave him. He seemed so lost and pitiful when he guessed we were thinking of doing that, once we crossed into Pennsylvania."

"And he doesn't have anyone else," Martha added. "He'd be found in no time. And our old owner, his own brother, would just shut him away in a madhouse for the rest of his life. He needs his freedom too." She sighed. "But sometimes, he is aggravating."

"He sure is!" Toby exclaimed, then hushed as his mother shook her head sternly.

Eliza smiled gently. "Well, there may be a quieter life ahead for all of you before long. Lucas should be back from Friend Scoggins's store soon."

Strad and Martha exchanged eager glances. Their eyes lit up at the sound of footsteps. The outer door opened and a man entered.

Eliza had risen. "What did thee find out, Lucas?"

Her husband, a bulky, boyish man, paused to rub his hands over the stove. "The best news in the world! Friend Scoggins says he'll be most pleased to have our friends here look after his second farm. He's been hoping to find good tenants since the last ones moved west to Minnesota."

"That's wonderful!" Martha exclaimed. She seized Strad's hand. "Did you hear that, Toby?"

Toby nodded. Lucas winked at him and walked to a bench along a wall where a game of checkers was set out. In a moment, Toby had joined him.

Eliza cleared her throat to get her husband's attention. "You spoke together privately?"

"Few people were about." Lucas looked up, smiling, and spoke to Strad. "I think you'll be happy there. It's rich land with five acres of apple and pear orchards. And Friend Scoggins is a fair and generous landlord."

Strad smiled. "It sounds like we've landed in Heaven itself."

"Hardly that," Lucas told him. "Though there was a sort of clerical atmosphere to our talk."

The others looked puzzled; Eliza frowned. Lucas continued. "As we were talking in the store, two brothers, ministers of the Gospel, approached. They seemed very interested in your case."

"Isn't that fine!" Martha said.

Eliza shook her head. "Their 'case', as thee calls it, should have been discussed in private."

"But Friend Scoggins was alone in the store, and I had to get back here," Lucas explained. He moved one of the checkers, then stopped when Eliza cleared her throat.

"Ministers of the Gospel?" Strad demanded. "How would they know about us?"

"I don't know," Lucas admitted, "but they did seem to, and even about Mr. Prendergast."

"What were they like?" Strad asked sharply.

"Oh, quite well dressed," Lucas said, "more so than most country preachers. They had fine black coats and one was very plump and comfortable. He laughed at everything. The other was thinner and much more serious."

"Were they asking questions?" Strad's voice was very dry.

"Not really. They seemed to know about you already. They just asked if Toby here—they didn't know his name—would be able to get an education at last, and I told them we had a fine school. That seemed to make them happy."

"Did it?"

"And they asked about Mr. Prendergast."

Eliza drew in her breath. "Too close!"

"Did they know his name?" Strad asked.

"I think so. Is his first name Leander?"

"That's right."

"That was a little strange," Lucas said. "The plump one started to say the name, but his brother shut him up."

"And what did they call themselves, these brothers?"

"Good names for ministers," Lucas said with a small laugh. "Blessington: they were the Blessington Brothers, they said, Henry and Norman."

Strad struck the table. "Those aren't preachers! Those are the Brimston Brothers, Hubert and Norton Brimston!"

"But who are they?" Eliza cried.

"They're slave-catchers. They're like devils, folks say. They can read the minds of black people. They know where we'll go before we do. And now they're after us!"

Martha had risen, clasping her hands together. "We have to leave," Strad declared.

Lucas shook his head in distress. "But this is a free state! And we've found you such a fine new home!"

"Remember those wicked Fugitive Slave Laws," Eliza said. "Our friend is right. We can't protect him."

"And like a fool, I believed them!" Lucas cried. "They seemed so honest, so friendly!" His colour rose. "Maybe *they'll* need to be protected if they try to seize you!" Then he saw his wife's gaze and bit his lip.

"Be calm, Lucas," Eliza said quietly. "We can't undo what's done. But we can set our friends on their way to a safer place. Thee'd be best occupied putting their horses to their carriage; at least the poor animals have had a rest. We'll tell you how to get to Philadelphia by the back road," she added to Strad. "You should be safe there. There are so many black people, and most of them are free under the law. I think you can pass unnoticed."

Strad just nodded. He and Martha quickly gathered a few clothes. Lucas gave the checkers and board, in a box, to Toby. Strad and Martha exchanged looks, then Strad went into the next room and returned with Li'l Massa. "We have to leave, sir," he told him.

"Must we always keep moving?"

"We do have to. But we may settle down in Philadelphia."

Li'l Massa looked with longing around the kitchen, at Eliza and Lucas. "I had hoped to find some quiet here."

"Well, sir," Lucas told him, "thee could surely stay here if thee wished. I'm sure we could find some proper occupation."

"No, no," Li'l Massa replied, frightened. "I must stay with my servants." Strad and Eliza exchanged glances but did not try to argue further.

The scene faded. The letters over the next scene read:

EVEN IN PHILADELPHIA
THE FUGITIVES WERE NOT SAFE:
AT THE GARDEN PARTY
OF DR. AND MRS. PICKERSGILL

The screen showed a garden on a warm day in Indian Summer, and a mellow brick wall; red and golden leaves drifted onto the shoulders of white ladies and gentlemen. Beside a hedge, Toby was standing with a large dish of fruit and bon-bons. Several ladies smiled at him; some patted his head while they made their selections. A small circle of guests surrounded an imposing, tall and stout black clergyman, addressing him as "Bishop Bromley". Strad and Martha moved decorously among the crowd, he with a tray of glasses, she with a wide plate of canapés. Just after they left the scene, two white ministers, one stout, one tall and thin, entered from the other side and began to move towards the bishop, whose hands they shook warmly.

At this first sight of the Brimston Brothers, the audience around Amos let out an angry sigh; Toby looked up from his fishing, annoyed, then looked down into the well again.

On the stage Norton Brimston, the plump one, was addressing the bishop. "We so admire the work you are doing!"

The bishop bowed. "Thank you so much, sir."

"We must visit your church!" added Hubert Brimston, the tall thin one. "We understand it is a real haven for escaped slaves." The bishop bowed modestly.

"We could learn so much there!" Norton added eagerly, and was rebuked by a look from his brother.

"It's these terrible Fugitive Slave Laws," Hubert said. "We've heard that wicked men can even come north to return the former chattels to their vile captivity."

"That's only too true," the bishop said, "but we keep a good lookout for such scoundrels."

"We're sure you do," Norton said with a smile.

Hubert coughed in warning and laid his hand on his impetuous brother's arm. "We have an extraordinary interest in your methods of keeping the fugitives safe. Our own congregation, in upper New York State, near the Canadian border, has provided shelter to a few worthy families, but they still fear recapture."

The bishop shook his head sympathetically. "How splendid it would be if we could bring them a message and advice from you!" Norton said.

"Why, we would be most pleased," said the bishop. "We can fix a date now." He drew a small notebook from his pocket.

While this conversation was going on, Strad had re-entered the scene with a fresh tray of glasses. He saw the Brimston Brothers and stood stock-still. Then he turned his head and whispered to Martha, who had just entered. With her tray of canapés, she made her way to Toby. They each set their trays down on a stone bench and left the garden, with Strad quickly but quietly following them.

Now the host, Dr. Pickersgill, an imposing bearded gentleman, and his aristocratic wife joined the group. The brothers turned towards them eagerly.

"Oh, Dr. Pickersgill, we want you to know how much we admire Bishop Bromley's splendid work, and your support of it!" Norton exclaimed.

Dr. Pickersgill looked at him, enquiring but friendly. Hubert raised his hand. "I am Henry Blessington and this is my brother Norman. When we heard of your benefit party on behalf of the bishop's work, we couldn't refrain from coming."

"And making a contribution," Norton added, a small roll of bills in his hand.

"Please!" said the host. "The young lady at the table behind the rose garden looks after all that. You gentlemen are most welcome. But I fear His Grace's glass is dry." He looked around. "Where can our waiter have gone?"

"Yes," his wife added, "where *are* those lazy dark—those lazy things?" She looked reproachfully at her husband. "I was afraid they'd be some of the flighty ones."

"Who was so flighty?" Hubert asked. "We couldn't help overhearing."

The host laughed. "Oh, nothing. A couple we hired to serve at this gathering, a man and a wife. They seem to have suddenly remembered business elsewhere."

Norton Brimston sighed. "Likely they didn't want to wait on a man of the bishop's colour, despite his high position. There is still ample room for your good example."

"It couldn't have been that; they were black themselves. I wonder if their son is still here...no, he seems to be gone too."

Norton Brimston giggled slightly. "Really! A black man and his wife and son, and they all just disappear in an instant. Perhaps they went home. Do you happen to know where they live, sir?"

"Not really," said Mrs. Pickersgill. "We found them through an agency. They were staying at some rooming-house, they said. But they were with an old white man—I've seen him several times, on a park bench near Walnut Street." He shook his head sadly. "A bit of a vagabond, though he *was* white."

"Wonderful!" Norton Brimston said.

Hubert Brimston added quickly, "My brother is always deeply touched to hear of our poor black and white brethren sharing their hardships. After all, even vagabonds are God's creatures. Perhaps we can comfort this one. Come, brother." They left quickly, stopping to smile at each guest they met.

Then the stage darkened, but the banner still glowed above, with the words:

THE PURSUIT CONTINUES

Strad spoke out of the darkness. "That's what happened—the chase continued. Those two really got after us, but at least we took them away from the flock of that dumb Bishop Bromley."

"I saw Julia, the cook, on our way out through the kitchen," Martha added, "and I just had time to tell her who they were."

"But those brothers gave us no rest," Strad said. "We were travelling light by that time. We'd had to sell the horse and carriage—luckily Li'l Massa didn't make any trouble over that—and we'd thought we could settle down a little, getting the kind of work you saw. But after that garden party we had to make tracks again. We hardly stopped to sleep or breathe."

"Hey!" Toby called from the well, "I think one's after my bait!"

"Well, don't scare it off," Strad called softly. He continued his tale in a lower voice.

"We went across country every which way, but we couldn't shake them. When we walked down a country road, we'd have to jump into the bushes while they rode by on fast horses. Once we slept in a barn, and we were lucky we got up before dawn; we looked back from the woods and saw them in that same barn, with other white men, sticking pitchforks in the hay.

"So we kept heading north, towards Canada. We knew they couldn't get us back from there. Some folks told us of easy places to cross, along the Detroit River, but that seemed too far and too dangerous. Straight north was the only way to go, even with all that big lake, Lake Ontario, to cross over."

Then, to solemn music, these words appeared on the banner:

AT THE GATEWAY TO THE PROMISED LAND

Dim light on the stage revealed the interior of a mean hut on a windy night. Rain lashed the windows, black drops of water seeped through. Strad's family sat at a table near a small, smoky wood stove. At one end of the table slept Li'l Massa, hunched over a bowl of porridge. Another man entered the room, a lean, bent white man with a black sweater and black cap. He had clearly been drinking, and as he sat down he drew a flat bottle from his jacket and took a long swig.

"Will this wind let up, Captain Perkins?" Strad asked him.

"I didn't order it," the captain said. "I can't send it back."

"But is the voyage safe? Will your ship make it across?" Martha asked anxiously.

"It's made it lots of times before. If you think you can find a better ship than the *Whiskyjack*, go out and find one. I've got people to see on the other shore—I sail tonight." He got up and stomped out of the cabin.

Strad looked at Martha and shook his head, "The man seems to think it's safe enough."

"I heard him. But Strad, it's such a dreadful storm."

"I wouldn't choose to go with the weather like this, whatever he thinks," Strad told her. "But those slave-hunters are right on our trail. They must be."

Martha sighed. "You're likely right."

"I'm sure I am. We'd better talk to Li'l Massa." Strad touched the sleeping man on the arm. "Sir! Sir! Wake up!"

Li'l Massa raised his head, a spot of porridge still on his nose. "What? What?"

"Massa," Strad told him, "we have to go across the big lake now. And Captain Perkins has kindly agreed to take us."

"It's the middle of the night," grumbled Li'l Massa. "Anyway, I don't like the man's looks."

"Massa, I think Captain Perkins is a good sailor, whatever else he is. He'll get us across somehow or other. But, Massa...."

"Where are we going?"

"Massa, the boat's goin' across to Canada. We're goin' there with her. But they's no call for *you* to go with the wind so high. Can't you hear those big waves?"

"An' it's a small boat, Massa," Martha added.

Li'l Massa looked from one to the other. "You're trying to escape again, aren't you?"

Strad and Martha looked at each other.

"No sir, Massa," Strad said patiently, "we ain't tryin' to 'scape. We just wants to go to a better place. Where we don't have to run all the time."

"That's right, Massa," Martha said. "Here we can't sit still. You've seen that. You've seen how them folks is always chasin' us. That's no life."

Li'l Massa looked at them in dismay. "You just want to escape *me*, then. I thought I could rely on you."

"We're trying to do the best we can by you, sir," Strad told him. "We'd like to keep you with us. But that's a mighty big lake out there. The waves is like castles. I never see water like that before. The sailor-man says he can get across, but I think he's a man who enjoys danger. Still, he's all we got. We three got no choice."

"But you can't go away and leave me!" Li'l Massa said. "I'm coming too."

For a moment, neither of the others spoke. Then Martha said, with resolution, "So, let's get dressed warm. That wind will be cold on the lake."

They put on thick sweaters and tied scarves
round their hats. Captain Perkins returned, wearing a
sou'wester and carrying others for his passengers. As
soon as they were dressed, they followed him out to a
small, tossing sailboat with one mast and a boom. Li'l
Massa and Toby huddled in a corner, trying to stay out
of the way, while Martha could not take her eyes off the
fierce waves crashing on the shore. The captain took the
tiller and shouted commands to Strad, over the roar of
the wind. With sail half-raised, the boat lurched away
from the pier.

The scene shifted to a small, neat house with nautical
decor, under the title:

MEANWHILE, ON ANOTHER PART OF THE LAKESHORE

A stocky, bearded man was serving rum to the Brimston
Brothers. By a large, hot stove a short, unshaven white
man, far gone in liquor, sat talking to himself.

The stocky man looked out the window. "It's a poor
night for it. You must want those people pretty bad to go
out after them."

"Oh, we *do* want them, Captain Barnabas!" Norton
Brimston burbled.

"Ever so much," his brother added, clenching his
teeth.

"Well," said the captain, "you're paying me pretty
well for this trip. And Dawkins there, he don't mind
what he does. He was a blackbirder, you know—that's
what they called the sailors in the old slave trade."

The short man by the stove belched. "Three thousand
slaves I ferried over from the horn of Africa," he said,
with a strong English accent. "Till finally it got too
dangerous even for me. The others showed the white

feather when the King of England forbade the traffic. You could hardly make a run without having the navy down your throat, boarding your ship and searching it stem to stern." He spat on the stove, which sizzled angrily. "But we had ways of getting rid of the evidence: just link 'em in chains with a good heavy anchor on the end, and dump them overboard when the warships got too close." He hiccupped and took another drink. "You could get rid of all the evidence except the smell. And they never hanged a slaver because of the smell."

"I can see you're the right sort!" Norton Brimston exclaimed admiringly.

"Never mind that," his brother said. "You'll have to put up with the smell for a bit, when we catch this lot." Dawkins only smiled.

"You seem mighty determined," Captain Barnabas remarked to Hubert.

"Determined! Yes, I am. We always catch what we chase. For these to get away! And not just a single man—that I could stand—but a whole family. A wife and a child and a crazy old white man to slow them down. Why, I'd never be able to look myself in the face again!"

Norton Brimston, a little disconcerted, added, "My brother takes this one very personally. We both do, of course."

Hubert snarled, "Personally! We've sworn to catch them, do you understand? We've both sworn!"

"You *made* me swear," Norton muttered.

"We've followed them this far," Hubert growled, "and we'll follow them wherever they go, until we lay hands on them. We'll follow them to Hell, if need be."

Suddenly Dawkins spoke. "All this talk, cap'n, and the blacks are gettin' away. Suppose we go see." He rose unsteadily and stumbled towards the door. "We can outrun Perkins's boat in any weather. And you know which way they're going—they have no choice. By dawn you'll spot them."

Captain Barnabas nodded. He put on his sou'wester and went out without a word. The Brimston Brothers followed, already dressed for wet weather, picking up two rifles and a shotgun as they went.

The scene shifted to an endless expanse of stormy lake under a cold grey dawn. The waves seemed to reach for the church roof, and the fierce whistling of the wind made the audience shiver. There was no land in sight anywhere. Then a small thinning grew in the greyness, and the outlines of the *Whiskyjack* came into view. Captain Perkins, at the tiller, was shouting to Strad, who was by the mast.

"That's Falcon Island!" the captain cried. "If we can get to the lee of that, we'll be safe!"

Strad nodded and crawled up to the others, in the bow, to tell them.

"Look!" Toby cried.

In the distance a second boat had appeared through the gloom, a larger boat with two masts, riding under shortened sails. As it grew nearer, all the watchers could see the word *Puritan* on its bow, with Dawkins's face above it. Captain Barnabas was at the wheel. The Brimston Brothers were crouched down, their white faces showing above their black sou'westers as they scanned the sea eagerly.

"There they are, Captain!" Dawkins cried. "Look at them, the blackbeetles, trying to crawl away into their crack!"

"Let out the foresail!" Captain Barnabas called. Dawkins ran aft to the ropes. In a moment the *Puritan* lurched ahead, plunging dangerously but gaining on the

Whiskyjack. Back at the bow, Dawkins whirled a grappling hook over his head and cast it at the smaller boat. It fell short. He drew it in for a second try.

Norton Brimston aimed his shotgun at the *Whiskyjack*, but his brother knocked down the barrel. "It's too far!" he yelled. "And we want our meat alive!" Norton grinned.

The *Puritan* drew closer still. Dawkins cast the grappling hook again but Strad knocked it away with an oar. Then, as Dawkins drew back for another cast, the foremast of the *Puritan* snapped. The *Whiskyjack* pulled away.

Amos started to cheer, but Strad's hand restrained him.

Before them, the larger boat had slewed around and waves struck it from every side. But the smaller boat was in trouble too: the waves seemed to tower over its mast. An especially big one gathered the boat up and dumped it on its side. It righted itself, but then another wave struck it, then two more, and it was swamped. As Captain Perkins struggled to control the tiller, Strad, Martha, and Toby clung to the mast over Li'l Massa, holding on to each other. Martha was praying, but her words were lost in the crash of the sea.

Flying spray hid the scene. When it cleared, both boats were capsized, and waves broke without restraint over their upturned keels. At first there was no sign of life. Then, by the *Puritan*, a long, thin white hand clutched at the air and disappeared into the dark, freezing water.

CHAPTER NINE

Captain and Guide

The image on the screen faded; the lights in the church came up again. The audience got up and stretched. Li'l Massa had also risen to his feet, and now he rubbed his hands together in satisfaction. "Well, we *did* get away, didn't we?" he exclaimed, as if the thought had just struck him.

Strad smiled. "Yes sir, we did. You already knew that."

Li'l Massa looked at him, puzzled, but only repeated, "We did get away." Suddenly he looked around him, at all the smiling black faces, and added, "But where do I go next? Where do we all go next? Are we always to be stranded on this bank and shoal of time, this backwater?"

"Gee," Amos said. "It doesn't seem so bad! *Sir*," he added, for Li'l Massa was staring at him in amazement.

"The boy's right, Massa," Strad agreed. "'Course, he's new here. But we know we're not here for ever. We just have to be ready for what comes next."

"Whatever that is," Li'l Massa muttered gloomily.

The soldiers stretched again and yawned. Amos thought, "It's just the way people act at the end of a movie." But these people were all dead, all spirits. He didn't think of them as ghosts; they weren't scary at all. They just lived in a different world—and he had come into theirs, not they into his.

He was more worried about Mr. Prendergast, Li'l Massa. Those Brimston Brothers were after him! Amos drew Martha aside where the others couldn't hear them. "Are those slave-catchers really devils from Hell now, or is that just a story?"

"Oh mercy, child! Here we don't know what's real and what's a story. We think we'll know when we get to the other side. Let's just say that they *think* they're devils, and the powers that be, the ones that call themselves the Central Office, let them act like devils." She smiled sadly. "Maybe all their wickedness comes from *your* world and they aren't able to leave it behind."

"But what do they want with Mr. Prendergast—with Li'l Massa?" Amos asked.

"How can we tell what such things want? They must be real empty, and they need whatever souls they can get to fill them up. And Li'l Massa thinks they're devils too, so we have to keep him out of their hands. Somehow, we're sure they have no real power over us, but if we don't look after him like we should, we may have to stay here in this halfway place, or a worse one, for a long time yet."

"Hey!" Toby yelled from the well. "I really caught a big one! That new bait works like a charm!" Strad and Amos joined him at the well, where he was releasing a dark brown bottle from his casting grapple. "Look here," he told them, pointing to its surface.

"That's right," Strad said, "it's as if a little boat was moulded in the glass when they blew it."

"And there's something dark swirling around in there." Toby shook the bottle. "I bet it'll come out soon."

"Now, you put that down!" Strad told him. "You break that now, the poor thing will be in all *kinds* of trouble. You just set it on a shelf and let it get ripe."

"What happened to the bait?" Amos asked as Toby carefully placed the bottle on a low shelf.

"The letter A? It's gone. I bet he swallowed it. Maybe we'll get it back later. But like my dad says, we better let it rest. I'm sleepy, too."

Toby showed Amos two bunks on the other side of the church. Strad was walking towards a curtain at the back of the kitchen, to their bedroom, where Martha had already gone. The soldiers were lying down on the church benches, covering themselves with their long coats. Only Rufus Palfrey, who was keeping watch, stayed awake. He carried the armchair back before the fire and sat in it, his feet up on a log.

Amos felt suddenly sleepy. He was annoyed at first: he didn't want to miss anything. But so much had happened since he had come into the old house. It must be way past his bedtime; he just couldn't stay awake any more. He looked around the old church, at Toby, who was already snoring, at the flickering firelight on the wall. He smelled the wood smoke. It would all be there when he woke up. He took off his glasses and lay down.

He woke to a touch on his arm and saw Rufus Palfrey shaking him. "You have a visitor, if you want one," Rufus whispered. He held his finger to his lips and beckoned for Amos to follow him.

Rufus led him between the benches and the snoring soldiers to the back of the church, then to the door of the bell tower. They climbed past the window through which he and Toby had watched the Brimston Brothers. The sky outside was still quite dark, but light was coming down the stairway. The next platform was full of daylight. A large black bell dangled from a crossbeam, with the rope hanging only halfway to the floor, far beyond anyone's reach.

Rufus pointed to a window across the platform. "That's where you have to look," he said. Amos walked cautiously to the window and looked at the world outside. It was the one he had left! He saw the lake again, and a view of Port Jordan, and Lester Prewitt standing on the wharf, looking down at the water.

"Well, do you see him?" Rufus Palfrey asked.

"Sure." Amos looked closely at Lester Prewitt. But the old fisherman didn't seem worried or frightened. Strad had said he would be if he thought Amos was in danger. Maybe no one's told him how long I've been gone, Amos thought. But how much time had really passed?

The long shadow of a post on the wharf was about where it had been when he had entered the shed. It was almost the same time he had entered the house—or else a whole day later. But could a whole day have passed? Maybe time just wasn't the same inside the house as outside.

He watched Mr. Prewitt reach down for a line that dipped into the water, draw it up a few feet, and then release it. He looked back at Rufus standing behind the bell. "He's just fishing for his driftwood," he told the corporal. "He's not looking for me. Could he see me up here?"

Rufus Palfrey smiled. "Well now, you can find that out easy enough. You can just call out to that old fisherman down there. Of course, then you'd have to go down and open the door. It's never locked from this side. Likely you'd have quite a story to tell him."

Amos looked down again, and turned back to Rufus in confusion. "Is that what you want me to do?" he asked.

"That depends," Rufus said. "You see, we're wondering just what you're doing here. Like Strad said, did you come just to learn our story, or do you want to help us *tell* it? Do you want to be part of it? If you go out of the house now, who knows if you can come back in?"

Below, by the lake, Lester Prewitt scratched his chin and began to look up at the house. Amos drew back quickly from the window.

"That's what I figured," Rufus told him. He waited another moment. "Well, I guess we better get on with the story."

They descended the stairs, out of the evening light to an early dawn inside the church and a smell of bacon and coffee. Martha, Toby, and the soldiers were having breakfast. Strad had gone to take Li'l Massa his. He returned with a tray; shortly afterwards, Li'l Massa himself entered, drinking from a mug of coffee. The soldiers looked up in surprise as the old man sat on a bench by the fire, saying in quite a normal voice, "I felt the need of a little warmth this morning." He turned his back on the others and looked thoughtfully at the flames, then turned to them again.

"You made a good catch last night, I believe," he said to Toby.

"Yes, sir. A big one."

"Well done! Did you say there were some signs on it? Was there a message in it? A message for me?"

"I couldn't see inside it, sir." Toby walked to the shelf again. "But there's a picture of a boat on the glass, just as clear as clear! Maybe that means a captain for our boat." He shook the bottle.

Strad called, "Now, you leave that bottle alone, Toby. It'll come out in its own good time."

"An' the stopper's bulging, too," Toby said.

"Well, you *better* leave it till it's ready," Strad repeated. He added thoughtfully, "Sounds like something is going to happen, though."

Martha said suddenly, "But we can't make a trip with just a captain, can we? Don't we need sailors too?"

"We have some strong men here," her husband assured her. "I figure we can sail a boat if someone shows us how."

"But there's no boat!" Li'l Massa wailed. "Do you call that hulk out there a boat? Its sides were staved in long ago and the fish played tag between its planks. How can we all travel in it?" Then his voice became sour and suspicious again. "Or do you plan to go off and leave me here?"

"No, Massa," Strad told him.

"We *can't* go off and leave you, Massa," Martha added. "We came here together, we have to leave together. Even if we wanted to leave you here, which we don't, we wouldn't be allowed to. Those seem to be the rules: like it or not, we have to learn what the rules are."

Li'l Massa nodded, still restless and anxious.

Toby had been fidgeting. "Would you like me to read to you, Massa?" he asked. "From the Alice book?"

"Yes," Li'l Massa said, brightening. "I never knew that one before. My brother must have kept it away from me." He wrinkled his brow. "Or had it been written at that time?"

"I don't think it had, Massa. The date on it says *after* we came here." Toby had walked to a shelf by the well, below the one with the bottles, and picked up a book.

Amos read the title. "*Alice's Adventures in Wonderland*, and *Through the Looking Glass*!" he exclaimed. "Where did you get that?"

"It just turned up there one day," Toby told him. "That's where we find new books. I guess someone in that Central Office decides what to send us. But come on," he added, "it's daylight outside. We can sit by the water now."

Toby, Amos, and the soldiers walked out the door, followed by Li'l Massa, and sat on rough benches before the church. On the immediate shore was a very small wharf, beside the hulk of the old sailboat. The shore was empty, though there were a few small houses along what must have turned into Main Street, and then the old fort. He could see no people.

But the lake had certainly changed! It was now broken up with shoals and black rocks which had been hidden by darkness the night before. Falcon Island was still in place, but it seemed wider and deeper than when he had seen it his first day in Port Jordan, and it was covered with thick trees.

He looked back towards the town. "Isn't anyone else there?" he asked Toby.

"I don't think so. We think the only real things are the church and the lake. When we try to walk away from the house, we never seem to get any farther."

Li'l Massa giggled suddenly. "Like Alice in the garden. Why aren't you reading?"

"In a little while, Massa," Toby said politely. "Amos is trying to understand where he is."

"I wish him luck," Li'l Massa said.

Amos was looking over the nearer part of the lake. "There's Falcon Island. Can't you go there either?"

Toby shook his head. "Not till we get a boat. We're waiting till the boat is ready to sail. Look down there."

Jefferson White and Rufus Palfrey were standing by the hulk, pointing to the broken planks and shaking their heads.

"Was that the boat you came in?" Amos asked.

"That's the one," Toby said.

"It was washed up there." Rufus Palfrey had joined them. Amos looked at the wrecked boat, on whose stern the word *Whiskyjack* was still barely legible. Its bleached timbers shone like the driftwood Mr. Prewitt had dried out on his wharf.

Li'l Massa was also looking at the hulk in a friendly way. "Ah," he said. " 'It has suffered a sea-change into something rich and strange.' " He smiled, pleased with himself and the words.

Rufus smiled too and nodded to Jefferson White. "The boss is saying his poems again. It's a good day."

Li'l Massa straightened up, still pleased. "But why aren't you reading?" he asked Toby.

"What part do you want, sir? About the Cheshire cat again?"

"No, not that. Though I was fond of cats; I used to recite poems to my cat, which my brother thought was odd. And that Cheshire cat was a wise animal. He said to Alice, 'You must be mad or you wouldn't have come here.' That's how I feel about this place."

"But you're not mad, Massa," Strad told him firmly. "You never were. Sometimes you just *think* too much, and maybe back at the plantation you got a little confused and saw things that weren't there; but we thought what you saw was better than the things that *were* there. Here, you're about as sane as anyone."

"That's right," Rufus said, and the other soldiers nodded too.

"Well, you may be right. What I'd really like to hear," Li'l Massa continued, "is about Tweedledum and Tweedledee."

"Oh Lord!" Samuel Musgrave exclaimed. "Those fat men. They'd say *anything!*"

Toby found the place and started to read. Li'l Massa nodded gravely as he described Alice's meeting with the two strange brothers. Then he began to read their poem, "The Walrus and the Carpenter", which Amos remembered very well from Naomi reading it to him in the village. But after the third verse, Li'l Massa interrupted Toby. "No, go on. I want the part about the Red King sleeping."

"Yes, sir. Do you mean, ' "It's only the Red King snoring," said Tweedledee.'?"

"That's it," said Li'l Massa. Toby continued:

"Come and look at him!" the brothers cried, and they each took one of Alice's hands, and led her up to where the King was sleeping.

"Isn't he a *lovely* sight?" said Tweedledum.

Alice couldn't say honestly that he was. He had a tall red night-cap on, with a tassel....

"No, farther down," Li'l Massa said. "About his dream."

Toby read on:

"He's dreaming now," said Tweedledee: "and what do you think he's dreaming about?"

Alice said "Nobody can guess that."

"Why, about *you!*" Tweedledee exclaimed, clapping his hands triumphantly. "And if he left off dreaming about you, where do you suppose you'd be?"

"Where I am now, of course," said Alice.

"Not you!" Tweedledee retorted contemptuously. "You'd be nowhere. Why, you're only a sort of thing in his dream!"

"If that there King was to wake," added Tweedledum, "You'd go out—bang!—just like a candle!"

"I shouldn't!" Alice exclaimed indignantly. "Besides, if *I'm* only a sort of thing in his dream, what are *you*, I should like to know?"

Here Li'l Massa interrupted Toby. "It was lucky for Alice that the king didn't wake up, wasn't it?"

"Well, sir," Strad told him, "to me that just doesn't make sense."

"It does to me," said Li'l Massa. "Ever since I first heard that passage, I've wondered if I might be a creature in someone else's dream."

All the soldiers burst out laughing. "Massa," Jefferson White said as soon as he could speak, "please don't go telling that around or folks will think you *are* crazy!"

"It's a perfectly sound idea," Li'l Massa said with dignity.

"Excuse me, sir," Strad said, "but it can't be. If you're in someone's dream, we are too, and so is Amos. And he's from the real world. You're not in a dream, Amos, are you?"

"No sir, I'm not," asserted Amos, who had never felt so awake in his life.

They all looked at Li'l Massa, who said, "I still think the idea has merit, but there's no use our arguing about it. It came from a fine book, though," he told Amos. "I used to read a good deal. It made the world, such as it was, almost bearable. But somehow my books fell away when we came here. And my eyes tire easily. So now I have to rely on my little slave boy." He shook his head. "Reading is a wonderful thing."

"I know it is," Amos said.

"*You* know? But surely you can't read!"

"Sure I can!" Amos said indignantly.

Li'l Massa looked at him, very puzzled. "How can that be?" he asked mildly. "Toby only learned to read so he can read to me. Mind you, he reads very well. I don't think a white child could do better. Certainly not my brother's children; they had no use for books. They laughed at my interest in them and tore out the pages. They used to say," he confided to the others, "that it wasn't good for blacks to read; that it gave them ideas." He chuckled. "My family didn't realize that they'd be more useful servants if they *could* read!"

The faces of his audience hardened. Li'l Massa looked at them in consternation and dropped his eyes. "I'm going back to my room," he told Strad finally.

Strad made himself smile. "You can stay here for now, sir. No one comes out on the lake in daylight. Those devils will leave you alone."

"No," Li'l Massa insisted, "I'm going back. Don't follow me. I'm perfectly capable of finding my way without my keepers."

He re-entered the church, leaving Strad and Toby with sad faces.

"Is that right?" Amos asked. "Slaves couldn't read?"

"Lord, didn't you know that?" Strad said, but his mind was elsewhere. He whispered to Martha, "He was coming to be real friendly for a while. Then he went back to his old bad self."

"Not all the way back," Martha said, "but he still thinks we're his slaves. Never mind; the good feeling will come again. He had a bad upbringing, is all. I'll go in, in case he calls for me."

"He sure did have a bad upbringing," said Strad. He turned back to Amos. "In most places it was against the law to teach us. Like the man says, it gave us ideas."

"But how did you learn?" Amos asked Toby.

"I didn't exactly learn," Toby confessed. "One day, I just woke up knowing."

"The folks in the Central Office must have thought it was a pity he couldn't," Strad added. "So they just planted that knowledge in Toby's brain. Afterwards, he taught us too. Samuel Musgrave likes to read his Bible. Rufus there could tell you all about the War of 1812, that got him up here in Canada. But he *really* likes to read about the Civil War in the States, the one that happened after our time."

"We all read this and that, except for Josiah, who knows his letters but doesn't get much pleasure out of it. But even he loves to hear Toby read to Li'l Massa. And he takes in the words as good as anyone."

The church door opened and Martha stuck her head out. "All of you come in. Something's happening with that bottle!"

They all trooped into the church, Toby first, the soldiers bringing up the rear. "Look here," Martha told them. "That bottle is just about ready to pop. I was afraid it would wobble itself off the shelf and break, so I put it on the rug."

She pointed to the rag rug before the fire, where the brown bottle was now rocking back and forth with a life of its own. Toby knelt by it. "I think I see someone in there!" he exclaimed. "And now the stopper's pushin' itself out!"

"Hallelujah!" Josiah White exclaimed. "They can't keep him in there any longer!"

In another moment the stopper had risen out and fallen to the floor. Thick black smoke oozed out of the bottle, rose till it met the shelf above, then curled across the room in a single dense cloud. It followed a draft to the fireplace, then stopped, swelled, solidified, and changed in an instant to a tall, hawk-nosed black man in a blue sailor's uniform and captain's hat. On his chest hung Amos's letter A.

The sailor shook the last traces of smoke from his body, spun around on his heels, and looked keenly at the church and its inhabitants.

"A church!" he said at last. "*That* I didn't expect!" He looked round it. "*Calice*, it's Protestant! Where am I, anyway?" He strode to the door, opened it, stuck his head out, drew it back quickly, and closed the door again. "So, at last I can come into that house, eh?" he asked. "I can tell: this is where the old house was, even if it's a church now. I always knew it was a haunted house; but then, it has to be, if I'm here."

He laughed. "I wondered down there, inside that bottle, where I would go. Would I wander over the lake for ever, like some damned mist? Would I fly to Heaven on an angel's tail-feathers? I didn't think so!" He looked at the row of surprised black faces. "You, have you been here all this time?"

"I think so, Captain," Strad told him politely. "I think we've been here all *your* time."

"We have indeed, Captain," Rufus Palfrey put in. "We've seen you outside the house, when you wouldn't come in and the other men had to carry out the crates of bottles."

"I knew it wasn't my place," the sailor said. "Why are you looking at me that way, you with the mouth open and the glasses on your nose? Who are you?"

"Amos Okoro," Amos stammered. "Are you Pierre Johnson?"

The sailor straightened himself proudly. "*Captain* Pierre Johnson, of the good ship *Shulamite*. *Sacrement!* She was a beauty!" He touched his chest. "When I saw this letter from her map chest, I couldn't keep away." He turned back to Amos. "But how did *you* come to hear of me?"

"From Mr. Prewitt."

"From *Lester* Prewitt? Is he here too?" Amos shook his head. "He's still outside then," the sailor asked, "on dry ground, out of the water?"

"Yes, sir."

"Then you must be from outside too," Pierre Johnson said. "How did you come here?"

"Amos just came in the door." Toby had drawn close and put his hand on Amos's shoulder. "He seemed to know his way in."

"Humph," Pierre Johnson said, "he'd damn sure better know his way out, too."

"What's going on?" Li'l Massa had walked into the church and was staring at the new arrival in disbelief. "Oh Lord, not another one!"

"Not another *what?*" The sailor turned angrily towards the old man, making him retreat behind Martha.

"Massa here don't mean any harm, Captain," she said firmly. "He just don't know better."

" 'Massa'; you call him 'Massa'?" But Pierre Johnson's voice softened when he looked at Li'l Massa's face. "Was he really your master, then?"

Strad stepped forward. "I'll explain all that, Captain. This is Mr. Prendergast, Mr. Leander Prendergast, the little brother of the man who owned us. And Massa, this gentleman is Captain Pierre Johnson, who's come here for some good purpose. You said you wanted a message from the bottle, and I think he's it. I think he's come to take us on our last journey." He turned to Pierre Johnson. "We came here by water and we know we have to leave by water, sir. We were just waiting for a captain. Maybe you can make our boat sail again."

"Oh, Lord," Li'l Massa said. He turned and walked back towards his room, but only got as far as one of the benches, then sat down with his head in his hands.

"Well," Pierre Johnson said, "I see *some* things haven't changed."

"Captain," Strad told him, "they've changed more than you think."

"Hah!" said Pierre Johnson, but he didn't argue the point. "Now we have to see about a boat. All I saw outside was a wreck. Maybe we can make it seaworthy."

"Jefferson White here's a good carpenter," Strad said. Jefferson bowed modestly.

"He'll *have* to be a good one, from what I saw," Pierre Johnson said. "But let's have another look." He opened the church door again. "Well now, would you believe that?"

The others crowded to the door behind him and stood there, amazed. At the end of the small wharf—making it look smaller still—was a long low boat, slim and powerful, with a cabin covering two-thirds of its deck. It was painted black with white trim.

"Where did that come from?" Jefferson White demanded.

Samuel Musgrave looked at him reproachfully. "Where did *any* of us come from?"

Pierre Johnson walked out in front of the church. "That is nothing less than my old boat, the *Shulamite*! I came out, and she came up to join me." He peered keenly at the boat's smooth sides. "Not a mark on her! Who'd think now that she stove in her sides on an ice floe?"

"She's beautiful, Captain," Strad told him. "All she needs now is a mast or two. We should be able to get timbers from the church."

"Mast! What kind of boat do you think this is? She has two 200-horsepower engines."

"Two hundred horses?" Strad asked, bewildered.

"Never mind," Pierre Johnson told him. "They didn't fail me before; they won't now." He stepped towards the water's edge. "All we have to do is get in her and sail away. Across the lake, to whatever's on the other side." He looked at all of them, even Li'l Massa, who was timidly sticking his head around the door. "There'll be room for everyone, even for the white boy here." He laughed. "If we get hungry, we can use him for fish bait."

"Captain, we got to talk," Strad said. He drew Pierre Johnson aside and spoke long and earnestly to him.

"All right, if you say so," Pierre Johnson said at last. "You know the rules better than I do, but it still sticks in my craw." He looked around. "It just about makes me want to crawl back in my bottle."

Josiah Stone, who had not spoken for some time, said suddenly, "You can't do that, Cap'n, 'cept you got some of them little cakes or pieces of mushroom, like in the Alice book."

"What are you talking about?" Pierre Johnson said. But as Josiah Stone started to explain, he cut him off. "Never mind. I can see I've come to a different place." He looked out across the water. "And the lake's different too," he said, walking towards the water's edge. "Where did all those sharp rocks come from? You!" He pointed to Amos. "Who put those rocks there? Were they there in your time?"

Amos shook his head.

"They wasn't here this mornin', Cap'n," Josiah Stone volunteered.

"They just come up while we were inside," Samuel Musgrave added. "Maybe they were put there for us to get around 'em."

Shaking his head, Pierre Johnson walked onto the wharf, the others following him. He stepped lightly onto the deck of the *Shulamite*, which quivered, welcoming him. "She's ready to sail, all right," he said to himself. "But she has to find her way through all those rocks. Does any of you know the way through?" He turned and looked back at the others. "No, you couldn't; they're as new to you as to me. We need a pilot to show us a safe route out, for sure!"

Samuel Musgrave said solemnly, "The one who put those rocks in will send us a pilot too."

"Somebody better send a pilot," Pierre Johnson retorted. "I'm not risking *Shulamite*'s sides on those rocks without one."

While Pierre Johnson tugged his chin, thinking deeply, Amos heard a faint and distant sound of whistling. It drew nearer, coming from behind the church. He turned and saw old Mr. Stern walking over the field, a shining cane hanging from his arm. He hardly recognized him at first. Mr. Stern wore blue jeans and an old blue sweater and a bowler hat with a strip of white cloth around the brim. He continued to whistle cheerfully, and tunelessly. Then, as he came up to the church, he broke into song:

> And when the saints
> Come marching in,
> When the saints
> Come marching in,
> I'm gonna be among that number,
> When the saints come marching in!

"Hello, hello, hello, one and all!" he called cheerily. Suddenly he looked behind him and held out his cane horizontally. From somewhere, a green and black duck with a tiny knapsack strapped to its back came fluttering and landed on the cane. "Are you here too, *Liebchen*?" Mr. Stern said fondly, sticking his cane into the ground. The duck fluttered up and perched on his shoulder, nibbling gently at his ear and tilting his hat in the process.

Mr. Stern looked around, beaming, and Amos saw that the band round his hat read "Authorized Guide".

"Here is your Authorized Guide, come to guide you across the Great Waters!" Mr. Stern announced with a laugh. He stepped forward and shook Strad's hand, then the hand of each of the other men in turn; he patted Toby on the head, bowed to kiss Martha's hand. He saw Li'l Massa standing by the others, watching with amazement as he shook all the black hands, and he was on his way to greet Li'l Massa too when he saw Amos.

His face turned grey. "Why are *you* here?" he whispered in a shocked, despairing voice.

Strad stepped forward. "It's all right, Mr. Guide. Amos just came for a visit; he's not staying."

"Is that so? His presence here is only tangential, so to speak? It isn't part of the eternal scheme of things?"

Rufus Palfrey spoke up. "The boy just came to look, at first. But now I think he wants to come along, at least part of the way."

"Just part of the way?" Mr. Stern asked. "He can do that?"

"He'll have to wait years before he goes the rest of the way," the corporal assured him.

"Good! Then I'm glad to have him here now. So, gentlemen and lady, I've been informed that I'm your guide. I've been told we are to make a journey, the journey you have been waiting for so long: to the Other Side, or the Promised Land, if you prefer: where all ambiguity ends, where we will finally know what we only guess at now. You have a boat and a captain and" —he bowed modestly—"a guide."

"We need a pilot," Toby said.

"Guide, pilot; pilot, guide. Who counts?" said Mr. Stern. He pointed. "Is that fine vessel our ship?"

Pierre Johnson had been watching Mr. Stern open-mouthed. Now he said, "That's the ship. *My* ship, the *Shulamite*."

"Wonderful!" Mr. Stern said. He held up his hand. " 'I am black but comely, O ye daughters of Jerusalem, as the tents of Kedar, as the curtains of Solomon.' That's what the young Shulamite herself said. You can read it in the Song of Solomon."

Pierre Johnson said, "Are you really a guide?"

Mr. Stern tapped his hat, almost dislodging the duck. "It says so here, I didn't put that label on. I was at the Central Office just for a moment before I came here. They said, because *I* was guided out of danger through the mountains of Tyrol so long ago, I should become a guide now myself. And they gave me this official sign."

Everyone nodded respectfully.

"Listen," Mr. Stern added, "I've guided or piloted myself through some strange spaces before, and I finally piloted myself away from my granddaughter. This job should be a snap!"

"In that case, Mr. Guide," said the captain, who had been staring at him, "tell me what all these rocks are doing here and how we're going to get around them."

"Two very good questions," Mr. Stern replied. "First, why are the rocks here?" He raised a finger. His duck flew from his shoulder and landed on a post, watching him expectantly. "Obviously, they have not been placed here to prevent the boat's passage. Because those who were able to place rocks so suddenly also gave you the boat. If they wished the boat to be wrecked, would they have repaired it and given it? That would be a vain and malicious action, and a wise man said that the Almighty is subtle, but not malicious. We may assume that this also applies to the Central Office.

"Therefore," Mr. Stern continued (and his duck nodded back at him), "the rocks and islands were put there to challenge your skill as a sailor and ours as a crew. What is life, or even afterlife, without challenges?

"Finally, in answer to your second question, how are we to get around these rocks? We will simply sail between them. But who's *this* gentleman?"

Li'l Massa, who had drawn away, now approached closer. "At least you're a white man," he said, and held out his hand bravely.

A dead silence fell, but Mr. Stern just shook his hand and slapped his shoulder. "Not so white as you think, *boychik*! Maybe it's *you* needs the pilot, not the boat."

Strad cleared his throat. "There may be something in what you say, Mr....?"

"Mr. Stern!" the old man cried happily. "Which means Mr. Star. Now you have a star to guide you!" He drew himself proudly erect. Then, remembering the duck on his shoulder, he shrugged, dislodging it.

"Off you go, beauty!" he cried. "On board with you!"

The duck obediently waddled to the boat and flapped aboard, the contents of its knapsack clinking. "Those are all the supplies *I'll* need," Mr. Stern said.

CHAPTER TEN

The Voyage of the *Shulamite*

Then—in almost no time, it seemed to Amos—they were all on board the *Shulamite*. Martha had packed lunches in bags and boxes that Amos and Toby had carried on board. Toby had looked wistfully at his fishing pole, but his father had shaken his head. "You can't be sure *what* you'd catch out there," he'd said.

Of course, they were taking their books along: the "Alice book", three editions of the Bible (one in Hebrew, which no one had yet been able to read), Rufus Palfrey's *History of the American Civil War*, and *Wuthering Heights*, which Martha had received one day and had read quietly and happily.

They took tools as well, just in case: several axes, spades, boat-hooks, and ropes, as well as the soldiers' rifles. "We don't know what country we'll have to pass through before we reach really open water," the captain said. It was a pity, he added, that they didn't also have a cannon or a machine gun.

At first, Li'l Massa didn't want to go. He kept talking about their last terrible sailing voyage. But then he realized that he would be left alone in the house. He quickly packed three poetry books that had somehow accompanied him to the church, found a cracked straw hat, and bravely said he was ready.

When they were all gathered at the wharf they saw Jefferson White hanging rope ladders on either side of the *Shulamite*'s bow. "That was the guide's idea," Jefferson explained. "So you two boys can keep a close lookout for rocks as we go. The rest of us will be standing guard." He pointed to their rifles, stacked near the cabin, two long boat-hooks, and a shovel and pitchfork. "I guess we can keep this boat to ourselves," said he, "if those devils try to come on board."

The others walked down the rickety grey wharf and onto the *Shulamite*, which accepted them without a tremor. "What a boat!" Rufus Palfrey exclaimed. "Solid as a rock!" He and the others looked with surprise and admiration at the row of shining instruments and the gleaming brass compass in the cabin. Amos was able to explain the compass to Toby, who had not even heard of one; but other dials and switches and levers, almost as many as in the airplane cockpit the flight attendant had let him see coming from London, left him completely puzzled. He figured that Pierre Johnson would be too busy to explain them, and only hoped that the captain knew what they were for.

"Captain," called Rufus Palfrey from the bow, "this boat cable is padlocked to a steel ring in the pier."

"*Merde!* Is there a key?"

"I don't see a key, captain, or even a keyhole. But there is some writing on it. It says, 'Ring the Bell to Open the Lock'."

"The bell? What bell? The *Shulamite*'s bell?"

"It must be the bell in the church tower," Strad said. "The one they used to ring whenever slaves were escaping across the lake. Where did I learn that?"

"It was in one of the shows," Rufus said. "You remember, the writing said that the bell wasn't used any more now, and that anyone who rang it before he was ready to leave might be stuck here for ever. But this looks like the right time to ring it."

"If there's trouble, I'm going to sail off," Pierre Johnson warned them. "I've finally got my boat back and I'm not going to lose her again."

"We still have to ring it." Rufus glanced at Mr. Stern, who nodded. "Who'll do it? Jefferson, you're mighty fast on your feet."

Jefferson White looked back towards the church uncomfortably. "No," Mr. Stern said suddenly, "Amos will go." The others looked at Amos. "He's not going all the way with us," Mr. Stern continued. "If he gets left behind, he has his own place back there, in what they call the real world. Amos, are you ready to go?"

"Yes, sir," Amos said.

All the others made room for him. "Now remember, you be light and quick," Rufus Palfrey told him. "You know the way up there. You'll probably have to climb for the rope. Swing that bell till it rings good, but don't wait around to see what happens."

"And go now," Pierre Johnson added. "Once we get out of the harbour we have quite a ways to travel. We have to get past that island, too, and damned if it isn't getting bigger!"

All heads turned towards Falcon Island. It *was* bigger, Amos saw, no longer a dot but a blob. Could it be moving closer? But no—the trees on the shore were no bigger than before. So it must be that the island had actually grown. But he didn't have time to figure it all out. "Scoot now, boy!" the captain called. "Ring that bell!"

Amos sprinted into the church, past the fire that was still burning brightly, and the television set, now dark and silent. But he didn't have time to look around further. He pounded up the zigzag stairs that went round and round up the narrow tower. Past the first window he went, catching just a glimpse of the *Shulamite*, with those on its decks looking up eagerly at the bell tower. Then he was on the landing beneath the bell. The rope was still out of reach; he jumped for it but came nowhere near. But he saw that the belfry was walled with rough horizontal boards, with just enough space between them for his fingers and toes. He climbed up the wall, looking back at the end of the bell rope dangling four feet behind him. When he was a little above it, he threw himself backwards and caught the rope. As the first *bong!* sounded, the bell turned and pulled him up again.

He saw the spread of the lake, and Rufus walking down the pier with the end of the cable in his hand. Behind him, Falcon Island had grown larger yet. Amos dropped from the rope. As he ran downstairs, biting a splinter from his finger, he heard the bell ringing on with a life of its own.

But what had happened to the stairs? They were no longer in short zigzags. He raced down one long straight flight and caught a glimpse of a hall with tattered wallpaper, several doors opening off on one side, dusty windows on the other. Down another long flight and around a sharp turn, down a shorter one to the ground floor. Where were the church pews, the fireplace? He was in an empty shuttered entrance hall. He ran around a corner, saw an open door, and dashed through the rooms of the old house, out the door by the shed, and down to the wharf where the *Shulamite* was straining at a rope that Rufus was holding passed around a post. As Amos leaped aboard, Rufus released the rope and the boat surged away from the wharf.

Amos turned to look at where the Church of Paul and Silas had been, but instead there was only the old house, the House of the Good Spirits, looking as quiet as if it had always been empty. There was a flash of lightning under a low bank of clouds, and a shadow that might have been a church steeple disappeared upwards.

Now they were in among the first of the small islands, with the wider lake open before them. "We're on our journey!" Samuel Musgrave cried. "Praise Jesus, we have a guide to show us the way!"

Mr. Stern smiled slightly. "Many thanks, Samuel. But now, let's go ahead slowly. You boys get on the ladders and keep a good lookout for rocks. Captain, can you tell the rest of the crew what to do?"

Toby climbed down on the port side and Amos on the starboard. Pierre Johnson told the soldiers to stand guard around all the rails. He kept Strad beside him at the wheel, in case he had to leave it suddenly. Martha had found a stove in the cabin and was preparing a big pot of coffee.

Their way was not too difficult, but they had to keep their eyes open. "Watch out there!" Toby cried. "Steer to the right!"

"To starboard," Mr. Stern called to the captain. The boat changed course, away from red stone spikes that protruded like spears from the nearest shoal.

"More to port!" Amos cried. "And tell the captain to slow down; those rocks could slice right through us!" For a moment the sharp ridge on the bottom came close to their keel. Then the *Shulamite* slackened speed and bore left.

"Is it clear on your side, Toby?" Mr. Stern called.

"Yes, sir."

"It's not clear here!" Amos cried. "Nothing but more rocks; move it over to port!" The boat turned farther to the left. In a little while, Amos called, "All clear now."

Mr. Stern stepped to the bow. "I don't see any shoals ahead," he agreed, "but keep your eyes open."

In a few minutes he had called them up on deck. There were still plenty of islands, but they were sailing through safe, deep water. Martha brought out coffee for everyone. Even Li'l Massa stood on the deck, sniffing the fresh breezes. Martha stroked Toby's head. "You boys are ready to be pilots yourselves."

Josiah Stone had been watching the direction of their voyage from the sun. "Are you sure we're not heading back to the slave states?" he asked uneasily.

The other soldiers laughed. "Slavery's long gone, Josiah!" Jefferson White said. "You know that."

"I know where I come from, too. Mr. Guide, are you sure we're not heading back there?"

"I'm sure. Once we get around Falcon Island, I think we'll be in open water, and really on our way."

Josiah nodded, satisfied.

"Look there! What's that swimming ahead of us?" Toby cried.

Amos craned his head forward, around the bow. There was the very same tortoise that had led him into the old house. How had it grown so quickly? It looked as big as the sea turtles he had seen in pictures. At the sound of Toby's voice the tortoise turned its old head and winked, but it didn't change course. Rufus Palfrey came forward. "There's that tortoise again," he said. "I wonder what it wants."

"I bet something's going to happen," Amos said, "and the tortoise wants to watch."

Mr. Stern motioned to the captain and the boat slowed down. He sent Amos and Toby to the ladders again. The islands were coming closer, although the water between them remained deep. A large island blocked their path now, with channels on the left and right. The water seemed clearer in the right-hand one, though it was only twice the width of their boat, but as they approached it they saw the Brimston Brothers sitting on either side, resting their feet on the water's surface. Now Amos knew them by name: Norton, the fat one; Hubert, the thin one. Norton waved his hand eagerly. "Yoo hoo!" he called. "Yoo hoo!" And his brother sent a high laugh over the water, to glance off the *Shulamite*'s sides.

"Take the port channel, Captain," Mr. Stern called. "You boys get in the cabin. You're too close to the water." Toby and Amos climbed on deck and ran to the cabin, but Mr. Stern kept his position on the bow.

"Those are the ones, eh?" Pierre Johnson asked Strad.

"That's right, Captain."

"I'm not surprised. There was talk about them on the lake in my time. Some folk said they saw them perched on ice floes, asking to be rescued. They all said they had enough sense not to take them aboard." He chuckled sadly. "We figured people who told such stories had been sampling their own wares. Look, they're coming closer."

"Watch out now!" Rufus Palfrey called. "Jefferson and Josiah, you watch on the right and left sides. Samuel, you go to the back. I'll take the front." The soldiers, rifles ready, took up their positions round the boat. Strad put his hands on Toby's and Amos's shoulders. But Martha took up the pitchfork and stood beside Samuel Musgrave, pointing the tines at the Brimston Brothers, who were now gliding towards them across the surface of the water.

The brothers sneered at the pitchfork, and at Li'l Massa, who was standing beside Martha, dangerously close to the water. "Oh, Mr. Prendergast," they called, "are you letting women protect you now?" They quickly approached their cowering target. But the captain stepped back from the wheel for an instant, thrust out a long arm, dragged Li'l Massa into the cabin, and sat him down on the floor, out of sight.

The Brimston Brothers snarled. Then Norton regained his good humour. "Why, it's old Pierre Johnson. Did you know we called you Lucky Pierre?"

Pierre Johnson walked to the side and spat into the water. "Naughty, naughty!" Norton Brimston called. "You pollute the water to show your contempt. Your brother was much more of a gentleman."

"How did scum like you know my brother?"

Hubert Brimston laughed. "Scum indeed: as insubstantial as foam on the water. But your brother was really sorry for us. He was afraid—unlike you, who don't know what fear is—but he waded into the surf by Falcon Island to help us, when he heard us calling so pitifully."

"He looked quite comical, going under," Norton Brimston added. "He was so frightened. He saw that we were walking on the waves and he begged us for help."

"Possibly the fool mistook us for someone else," Hubert Brimston snickered.

Pierre Johnson threw a boat-hook at them. Hubert caught it in the air. The wooden handle burst into flame and was quickly consumed. He tossed the metal hook to his other hand and bent it in two over one finger. The tortoise, basking just astern, splashed the water with its forepaws, then dived.

"Don't try such tactics, Captain," Mr. Stern said quietly. "You're only doing what they want. It's our will, not our weapons, that keeps them away."

Norton Brimston went on with his tale as if he had not been interrupted. "But no help came. He went down, the poor fool. Then he came up again, up and out of the water and away over the sky."

"Where we're going now," Pierre Johnson said angrily.

"No fifty years in a bottle for him, like you spent because of your hard heart and your pride," said Norton Brimston.

"So we'll each have a story to tell when we meet again," Pierre Johnson said to no one. He returned to the wheel and the boat sped forward, leaving the Brimston Brothers behind.

Now the *Shulamite*'s path was clearer. The islands were far apart and the path to Falcon Island and the open water beyond seemed free and full of promise. And Amos and the others realized that the island had grown larger still. It covered most of the horizon now, with just a thin line of clear water showing on either side.

The vegetation on the nearer islands had changed, too. Live oaks spread their strong limbs, hung with great beards of Spanish moss. Living and dead cypresses stood in the brown water. Small fish swirled and jumped continually among the cypresses' bony knees. White cranes waded in the shallows, looking scornfully at the passing boat.

From around the next bend they heard the sound of music. The *Shulamite* came to the head of an island and in sight of another, which was dominated by a large white house. They could just see its top at first, and its wide roof, supported by four white columns.

"Oh!" Li'l Massa cried. He was still in the cabin, but had been looking out for some time.

"What is it?" Mr. Stern asked him.

"It's Alabaster Plantation, my old home. How did it follow me here?"

"That's right!" Strad cried. "Never mind, sir, you're in different company now."

But these words did not comfort Li'l Massa as much as they should have. "What will they think of me?" he whispered, so that no one but Mr. Stern heard him.

The *Shulamite* turned a bend, and the sound of music grew louder. Now they could see a happy party on the lawn before the Big House: southern gentlemen in frock coats, and belles in wide white and pink dresses. The

music, an elegant waltz, came from a small string orchestra seated between the two right-hand pillars of the
mansion. Magnolia trees showed their great blossoms;
redbud and plum blossoms ornamented the scene in red
and white. Li'l Massa gazed at it all with longing. Strad
and Mr. Stern watched him uneasily.

The Brimston Brothers, also in frock coats and with
the broad-brimmed hat and topper that Amos had first
seen, stepped through the dancers to the bank. "Oh, Mr.
Prendergast," Norton Brimston called. "At last you've
come! Your own people are waiting here for you!"

"Shall we send a boat, sir, to take you off?" Hubert Brimston asked. "It wouldn't be suitable for your
present company to join us here at Alabaster Plantation." He pointed to a small, gaily painted barge by
the bank which the tortoise was propelling slowly forward, his paws on his stern. "Our trusty servant can fetch
you easily," Hubert added. "Come back to your own
kind: to culture, to elegance. Your own brother bids you
welcome."

And sure enough, Ol' Massa himself stepped forward.
He wore a glossy black frock coat, and diamond buttons
glowed on his dazzling white shirtfront. He looked at
his younger brother with disdain. Then, at a cough from
Hubert Brimston, he smiled widely, as if in welcome.

"Dear brother Leander," said he, "I see you've been
travelling for your health. A sea voyage is always pleas-
ant. But surely, brother, your companions are unworthy
of you."

Li'l Massa had at first drawn back. But now he spoke
with more firmness than Amos had heard before. "A
gentleman should be accompanied by a proper retinue
of servants."

"What's that?" Pierre Johnson growled, but Mr. Stern
held up his hand to stop him.

Ol' Massa had heard the exchange. "Perhaps you've forgotten what properly trained servants are." He snapped his fingers and suddenly four smiling black figures appeared: a butler, two footmen, and a wide mammy in a white headcloth, all bearing platters of food and drink.

Li'l Massa looked at this lot with little interest. "I suppose you need all that," he told his older brother. "But I was always more modest than you. I have everything I need."

"Oho," Ol' Massa sneered, "you're quite a saint now, are you?" But Hubert Brimston pulled him aside and spoke in his ear, and when Ol' Massa spoke again his wide smile was back in place.

"But brother, you had such a taste for beauty and art. Surely you haven't given up your poetry?"

"Indeed not," Li'l Massa said. ("Well done!" Mr. Stern whispered in his ear.)

"I'm delighted to hear it. There is someone here who's been waiting to meet you."

He snapped his fingers again and a slim, languid lady in a spreading crimson hoop-skirt sidled towards the water, a limp black book in her hands. "This is Miss Havergail, our well-known poetess," Ol' Massa told his brother. "She has prepared some verses to welcome you here."

Miss Havergail coughed modestly, took up her book, and read:

Where the fair magnolias blossom,
And the darkies feast on possum,
That's where you'll find my old plantation home.

To a sweet romantic tune,
Beneath the Southern moon,
There I'll return, and never more will roam.

The eyes of Ol' Massa's servants were moist, and even Ol' Massa himself sighed. "Isn't that beautiful?"

"No," his brother said.

Ol' Massa's smile vanished instantly. "What do you mean, no?"

"It's wretched doggerel. Wherever did you dig it up?"

"I'll have you know that Miss Havergail commands the very highest fees for her presentations. She is a very successful poet!"

"Whatever she may be, she's not a poet."

The tortoise took his paws off the barge and dived, splashing the indignant Miss Havergail. She cried out in disgust, and was escorted back to the plantation house by Ol' Massa's dismayed servants.

Li'l Massa called into the cabin, "Captain, can't we move on?"

"Wait a moment!" Ol' Massa called from the bank. The captain looked enquiringly at Li'l Massa, who held up his hand while his brother spoke. "Enough of poetry, then. You'll agree that it leads nowhere."

Li'l Massa just smiled.

"Let's talk of reality," his older brother continued. "You are keeping company with stolen property."

"Stolen?" Li'l Massa asked in surprise.

Hubert Brimston spoke up. "Indeed yes! Those so-called soldiers in your boat—the poor fools were taken away by the British in the War of 1812. The *British!* The enemies of your country. That new little nigger thinks he's free, but we happen to know that we bought and paid for his ancestor—he cost us ten coils of copper wire and fifty pounds of nails—even if that black bitch, his aunt, stole him away again. You owe us for him!"

Li'l Massa looked at Amos, his face very troubled, and Hubert went on. "As for that family who used your own illness to make their escape, they stole themselves away from their rightful owner, your own brother!"

"They were *my* servants!" Li'l Massa retorted. "They still are."

"*Yours?*" Ol' Massa jeered. "What was ever yours? There isn't a court in the land that would dispute my claim. I hope you still have some respect for the law."

Li'l Massa, puzzled, turned to Mr. Stern. "Is that right?"

Mr. Stern cleared his throat. "Tell your brother the courts have changed. You may face other courts soon. I hate to think what they would say about both your claims to own these good people."

Li'l Massa nodded gravely and looked up at his brother. "My adviser says that neither of our claims is clear."

Ol' Massa's face twisted. "Your adviser! You've sunk pretty low to use a gentleman of his ilk! I'd have sent Ikey here to the back door to peddle his trinkets to the niggers."

Li'l Massa straightened up. "If you descend to insult, I have nothing further to say. Captain, please go on."

"About time," the captain muttered. The *Shulamite* moved forward. The occupants of the plantation followed after it with plaintive, hungry cries. The Brimston Brothers ran along the bank ahead of them all, leaving Ol' Massa far behind. They saw the tortoise's head grinning above the water and beckoned to it, but it swam away past the boat and was soon out of sight.

The path along the shore ended and the Brimston Brothers were brought up short. "Off you go; off with your niggers, with our niggers," Norton Brimston called to Li'l Massa. "We'll get you yet!"

Li'l Massa looked around at them. "There's another white man here," he announced proudly.

The brothers stood together at the foot of the island, holding onto each other, rocking with laughter. "It depends on what you call *white!*" Hubert called as the

Shulamite pulled away. "And anyway, wait till you hear what *he* did!"

Then the brothers could pursue them no farther. They stopped at the foot of the island, while the *Shulamite* pulled away.

There were more islands ahead, around which they would have to sail, but Falcon Island was almost in full view: its palm trees—palm trees!—and beach and its high hills, which had not been there an hour before.

The space between the nearer islands was so large that now there seemed little reason to keep a sharp lookout for the bottom. Mr. Stern called the boys, who had started to dangle their bare feet in the water, back on deck, and the *Shulamite* surged forward through the salty air.

The salty air? The captain noticed it first and sent Toby to the bow ladder to dip up a can of water. He tasted it and spat it out. "This is seawater," he announced. They all turned to look at the shore from which they had come. But there was no sign of the lake, or the town, or the old house. Only islands, with large birds flying over them. Grey pelicans perched on decayed stumps along the banks, gazing at the travellers dubiously.

"Look there, Cap'n!" Toby cried. The way, which had seemed so open, was blocked again; this time by a sandbar between two widely separated islands. The water was clear again; they could see that where the middle of the bar dipped under water there might just be room for the *Shulamite*'s keel to clear. But on the right-hand side of the passage stood the two Brimston Brothers. They were now dressed in gleaming white suits with broad-brimmed straw hats.

The captain slowed the ship's engines and set the guards in their places. Mr. Stern again sent the boys to the cabin. With his feet on the starboard ladder, he guided the boat by hand signals.

Li'l Massa looked enviously at their new clothing and sadly at his own stained garments. But for a moment the pursuers were paying no attention to him.

"Oh, Ikey," Hubert called.

"Mr. Stern to you," the guide answered.

"Ooh," Norton crooned, "aren't we grand!"

"Were you so grand," Hubert asked, "when you followed your hired guide over the mountains of Tyrol and left your family behind in Vienna for the laundry-men?"

Mr. Stern had turned away to guide the ship. The *Shulamite*'s keel just kissed the sand, but he motioned it on. It kept moving, towards the deeper water ahead.

"How they sizzled in the ovens," Norton said. "I wish you'd seen them. "

Mr. Stern opened his mouth, then closed it again. Amos, who was watching from the safety of the cabin, looked from him to Li'l Massa, and was encouraged by the disgusted expression on his face.

Hubert Brimston had been watching Li'l Massa too. He said, "My brother has a grisly sense of humour, Mr. Prendergast, but he really means no harm. It's just his little joke. But seriously, your Mr. Stern, if that's what he calls himself, has shown himself to be nothing but a coward. He ran with no thought for anyone but himself. Turned his back on his whole family. And this is the man you look to for guidance!"

At that moment, the *Shulamite*'s stern cleared the sandbar. Mr. Stern signalled vigorously to the captain, who sent the boat surging forward. Its wake washed over the sandbar, lifting the Brimston Brothers off it. It was true that they could walk on water, but the new waves rocked them off their feet. They landed in the foam, their hats flying in two directions, their bodies spinning. The ship left them behind as it made a straight path towards Falcon Island.

"Ho for the deep blue sea!" Mr. Stern exclaimed. But his eyes were troubled.

Samuel Musgrave came up to the bow, looking disturbed. Li'l Massa followed behind, listening. "Mr. Guide," Samuel said, "is it true what those devils said, that you left your family behind?"

"I'm afraid so, Samuel. This was long ago, but to me it's like yesterday. It was in Vienna, in 1938, when Germany had swallowed up Austria for an appetizer before starting on the rest of Europe. I knew we should be elsewhere. Already the Nazis had painted a Star of David on my father's shop window. But still he couldn't see what was to come. My parents and my grandmother, *olav-ha sholom*, they were all such plump, good burghers, not used to travel. How could they walk over the mountains? They were so comfortable where they were. They said, 'We are good citizens, solid conservative citizens. It is unthinkable that we should come to any harm.' They were angry at me for frightening them. I had to go alone in the end."

Samuel Musgrave nodded. "Sure, Mr. Guide, I know you did your best. There was no way you could have set them free."

"I wish I could believe that," Mr. Stern sighed. "Maybe I should have argued more. Sometimes I think I really wanted them to stay behind, so I'd have a better chance to get away."

"Well, now you have a chance to get Li'l Massa through."

"Thank you, Samuel. What an exchange! But thanks anyway, and you too, Mr. Prendergast. I'll do my best for you."

The captain had listened closely to this conversation, while pointing his boat at the great island that filled all the space before them. "I always knew my boat could travel far," he said thoughtfully, "but I never knew just how far until now."

CHAPTER ELEVEN

In the Footsteps of the Tortoise

A hot tropical sun beat down on the lagoon. On the white sand beach, the palm trunks and fronds offered only a mockery of shade. The jungle behind, seen over the shining sand, was dark. A spicy, disturbing wind wafted out towards the *Shulamite* and her crew as the boat crept cautiously along the coast. Except for occasional strange, threatening bird cries from the jungle, the land was still.

Their guide and their captain had taken them towards land past foaming reefs, which were now well behind them. Looking back, they could see that the network of islands through which they had sailed earlier had disappeared.

How far would the shore before them extend? Could they eventually sail around this land, which they still called Falcon Island, but which, even at a distance, filled all the horizon?

The *Shulamite* came to another bend in the long coast, where a gentle bay opened up. It was fed at its base by a stream that flowed down over green and black rocks. Near the stream was a landing stage floored with bamboo.

"What do you think?" the captain asked Mr. Stern.

"We must be meant to land here," the guide said. "For whom else was this landing-place made? There may be a further sign for us."

The captain nodded, doubtfully, but turned the boat into the little bay. At Mr. Stern's directions, Amos and Toby watched the bottom—smooth sand with shoals of red and blue fish twinkling by. The water was still deep beside the landing-stage. Strad and Rufus Palfrey jumped out to tie up the *Shulamite*, and all the company trooped ashore.

Li'l Massa had been watching the shore with great interest. "What's that ahead?" he cried. He had been looking at the foot of the stream, where it fell over two large black rocks with a larger green one, fully six feet long, in the centre. The green rock was domed, symmetrical, and curiously mottled. It looked almost like a tortoise's shell; indeed, Amos had to stare hard to be sure the rock wasn't a tortoise. Then he leaped back: the tortoise stuck its head out, a head that was now as big as that of a man. He winked, nodded, lumbered out of the stream, and waddled over the dry sand to the edge of the bush, his wet track drying quickly behind him. He paused, bent his head back, and, unmistakeably, motioned to Amos.

Amos started forward, the rest following him. The tortoise shook his head peremptorily. "I think he just wants *you*, Amos," Toby said in a frightened voice.

Mr. Stern stepped forward and laid a hand on Amos's arm. "What do you say, *boychik*? I don't think he means you any harm. They tell me he brought you here in the first place."

"I'll go," Amos said.

"But you be ready to run, you hear?" Rufus Palfrey told him. "Jefferson, you walk the softest. You just follow a little after."

Jefferson White nodded. He and the others had left their uniform coats and hats behind in the tropical heat. Now he removed his boots, waited until Amos had followed Tortoise into the bush, and followed them. Amos could sense Jefferson's shadow flickering among the vines behind him.

The tortoise led him to a sun-dappled clearing under great trees, though still within sound of the surf, turned, and sighed heavily. "You are all to follow me," he said in a mournful, leathery voice.

"Yes, Tortoise," Amos said.

"You know my name," Tortoise announced, not especially pleased. "Do they know it too?"

"Everyone knows what you are."

Tortoise shook his head widely on his long neck. "They may think they know *what* I am, namely *a* tortoise. Only *you* know I am Tortoise. You have heard my stories." He waited importantly until Amos nodded. "Of course you have," Tortoise said complacently. Then he sighed, so that the ground shook. "I am a most unfortunate creature."

Amos had his own opinions about this but did not express them. Tortoise coughed modestly. "Yes indeed, my spirit always aimed higher than my body could take me. I wear my segmented shell with pride as a witness to my struggle."

"That's right," Amos said, remembering some of the old stories. "You kept falling out of trees and breaking your shell."

"What a way to put it!" Tortoise scowled. "I didn't only fall out of trees."

"Once you fell out of the sky, didn't you?"

"Humph," Tortoise said. "I begin to regret that I chose you to communicate my wishes to the others of your group. I thought you knew my story. It now appears that you may have heard some mistaken versions of it."

Tortoise swelled within his great shell and hissed, then withdrew his head. When it came out again, tears were in his eyes. "That is my fate, always to be misunderstood," he said. "Because of my intelligent and generous nature, it seems to be my punishment to lead groups such as yours through jungles such as this.

"But let there be no misunderstanding," he added, much more firmly. "Such *is* my duty now. Straight from the Central Office! All of you are to follow me overland, till we reach the sea again: not this sea, the more distant one on the other side of the jungle."

"How long will that take?" Amos asked him.

"As long as it does."

"I mean, the captain won't want to leave his boat again."

"Alas," Tortoise said, "none of us likes what we have to do. He won't let the rest of you go on without him."

Amos nodded. Tortoise turned around, leaving a large pressed place in the grass of the clearing, and started back to the beach. When they had almost reached it, Tortoise turned again and scratched at the earth with his hind foot. "Call your party now, including the one who's been following us. I'm eager to see the next episode in your story."

Tortoise didn't look so eager, Amos thought. In fact, he withdrew his head into his shell, from which soon emerged the sound of snoring.

Amos joined the others and told them about his conversation with Tortoise. Pierre Johnson shook his head. "I don't trust that critter. I don't see why we should do what he says."

"I don't know if it's a question of 'trust'," Mr. Stern mused. "Amos, you know more about the tortoise than we do. Can we believe what he says?"

"No," Amos told him. "You can't ever believe *ev*erything Tortoise says. But when he said he was told to lead us, I think that was true."

Pierre Johnson looked questioningly at Mr. Stern.

"I trust Amos's instincts," the guide said. "Also, I think we really have no choice." The captain nodded gloomily.

"We have to travel light," Mr. Stern added, looking affectionately at his duck, which was happily swimming in the cool pool at the foot of the spring. "Come," he called. The duck flew to his arms. Mr. Stern gently unstrapped its knapsack, removed the bottle, which was still half full, and threw it far out to sea. "It's never too late to change," he remarked to the duck, who was again perched on his shoulder.

The soldiers took their rifles; the other men carried axes, except for Li'l Massa, who found a machete and a broad-brimmed straw hat; Martha kept her pitchfork, and told the boys to carry the picnic lunches. Li'l Massa also looked over his books and, to Samuel Musgrave's relief, finally selected a Bible. Then they set off into the bush, to where Tortoise was sleeping.

And there they waited. Tortoise continued to sleep. His snores sounded so like the humming of bees that some golden and black bees flew out of a tree to investigate, then flew back, disgusted. Jefferson White picked up a stick. "I'll poke that tortoise awake," he declared. Then he dropped the stick as an angry head came snaking out.

"Disgraceful!" Tortoise snapped. "A fellow can't get any sleep around here!" He yawned, slid his head in and out of the shell, sighed loudly, and finally said, "Well, if we must, we must." He started into the bush; at first his

pace was so slow that the others had to make an effort
not to overrun him, then he reached a comfortable pace
for the humans behind him.

At the beginning, Toby kept running in front of Tortoise, and once even jumped on his back for a ride.
Tortoise stopped, put his head in his shell, and refused
to take it out until he was quite sure his rider was gone.
Strad told Toby sternly to keep off their guide's back.

All of them, including Amos, looked with wonder
at the strange bright flowers, the hanging vines, the
darting, colourful birds. From some branches, long mottled snakes hung down and looked at them with hidden
smiles. It was a jungle quite unlike the one by the village, Amos thought; perhaps it was a jungle designed by
someone in the Central Office, whatever that was.

And for the moment it was very silent: he could hear
only Tortoise's heavy treads and the footsteps of their
own party. But it was not a dead silence, rather one that
seemed full of life, ready to burst into song. All the party
walked without daring to speak, except for Tortoise, who
scolded and muttered to himself.

Li'l Massa, especially, looked at the bright colours
and life with wonder and joy. His eyes glowed and,
for the first time since Amos had seen him, he began
to whistle. All the others smiled at him; even Tortoise
stopped for a moment and looked back at the sound, but
then plodded forward with a look of deep disapproval
on his face.

Li'l Massa said to Mr. Stern, "I *like* this southern air.
It reminds me of the times I'd walk out in the woods
by the Big House, in the early morning, with all the
moist green around me and no thoughts but my own."
He smiled sweetly and added, "I made my own world,
or rather my own worlds, inside my mind. Everything
became a green thought in a green shade, as a poet once
said. I would take my sketch book, you know, and try to

draw, but I had no talent there. I was more at home with words, and wrote a few verses of my own. Would you believe that?" he asked Mr. Stern timidly.

"Why not? Besides, since you like other people's verses, you should make up some too."

"Really? You know, I never dared show them to anyone there."

Mr. Stern nodded. "I think that was wise. But here, no one would laugh. Why, I bet our friends here," he nodded around him, "would like to hear them."

"Our friends?" Li'l Massa looked very puzzled. "Oh, you mean my servants and the others. Those soldiers." He lowered his voice. "I'll tell you, I didn't want to ask where they came from when we found them in the church. I was never one to condone runaway slaves. *I'm* not an Abolitionist!"

"No," Mr. Stern agreed sadly.

Little by little, Tortoise had started to walk faster. Now he led them inland at such a pace that they found it hard to keep up. They were following an ascending trail, made by human feet, though they saw no other humans. They were higher than the jungle trees now, and from a hillside they saw, far away, a group of wooden huts among which a troop of soldiers, dressed in modern uniforms, was standing at ease. Amos stopped to stare at them, and the others gathered around him.

"What do you see, boy?" The captain held out his binoculars.

"Those are government troops," Amos said after a while. "I saw pictures of their uniforms in my Aunt Naomi's house in the village. She talked about them."

"What troops were they?" the captain demanded. Mr. Stern looked as if he didn't have to ask.

"It was in our war. They were real mean! Everyone was afraid of them." Amos watched the soldiers, who were carrying modern rifles. Row upon row of them were marching along a narrow path, with others beating the tall grass beside the path. "I sure hope they don't come after us!"

Tortoise chuckled.

"Well, we'd better keep moving," said the captain. "They're some distance yet. Besides, we're not concerned with their wars."

"We can't say that any more, not here," Mr. Stern remarked. "They'll probably decide if we're concerned or not."

Now their path began to show signs of war. They passed one burnt-out village, then another, in which, among the scorched timbers of huts, were also the carcasses of an army truck and a jeep. The occupants must have all fled.

But Tortoise was continuing their march so quickly that they had no time to look. They had been walking uphill for hours. Was it really hours? Amos wondered. The sun seemed fixed in the sky, at about three in the afternoon. When he mentioned this to the others, Samuel Musgrave said, "It's like Joshua holding the sun from moving."

Mr. Stern added, "Why should it move? Time will move when it has something to move for."

They came to the top of a hill and moved along a narrow ridge. The earth was stony here, with few trees. Often they could see wide vistas below them, valleys deep in jungle. Tortoise just kept moving. During the last part of the voyage, he had hardly spoken to them. Amos, right behind him, heard him complain to himself from time to time, especially when the path was steep and rocky. They reached the crest of the ridge, from which they could see over three valleys; there was no hint of the sea in any direction, but there was a speck in the sky that grew larger as they watched. Tortoise stuck his neck far out and said, "Now they even make *machines* that fly!

And I, who once tied feathers to my arms and mounted to the sky to trick the birds—I am only an earthbound messenger."

But they were all too busy watching the airplane to pay attention to Tortoise's speech. It was a small plane with a single propeller, the kind Amos had seen pulling a banner above the lakeshore advertising a fair in Port Jordan. But this one wasn't pulling a banner. Someone was firing a machine gun from it into the jungle. As the plane turned along the valley at the foot of their ridge, they could see flashes from the gun barrel. "Aunt Naomi told me about planes like that in our war, too," Amos said.

Now the plane flew up to the level of their ridge and past them. The Brimston Brothers, suddenly sitting on either wing, waved at them. Norton Brimston called, "Yoo hoo! Yoo hoo!"

"I figured we'd see them again before long." Rufus shook his head. "I don't know what Heaven's supposed to be like, but at least I figure we won't see *them* there."

"Amen to that, brother," Samuel Musgrave said fervently.

Tortoise had stopped for a good long time to watch the airplane, and stayed motionless even after it disappeared over the next hill. "A much over-rated skill, that flying," he muttered, starting down the path at last.

Amos explained to Toby that Tortoise, in the old stories, had been up to the sky more than once, getting there by ropes or by wings, but that he kept falling down to Earth. This was why, the stories said, his shell was so cracked. It hadn't improved his temper, either.

"Look!" Toby called, "we're on a road now."

He was right: the path had widened to a dirt road, much rutted with tire tracks. They came upon a burnt-out bus, fortunately empty, as they descended, then a pickup truck, its cabin pitted with bullet holes, the back full of rotting mangoes under a black cloud of flies.

From below acrid smoke reached them. A bend in the road showed them a large town in the valley. Tortoise waddled off the road to a bare field on the right which gave a panoramic view of the town. Smoke rose from several burning houses and from a burning gas station. Almost directly beneath them, for the hill was very steep here, was a market, most of whose stalls were empty. A band of government troops marched through it, stopping to thrust their bayonets into bundles of cloth in one stall and piles of apples in another. Only one stall-keeper remained, a woman with a red headcloth who offered pineapples to the departing soldiers.

Tortoise watched all this with interest. He straightened his short legs, so that they could see the sky beneath his shell, turned to the road again, and started down the hill.

"We goin' down *there?*" Josiah Stone cried. At his words, a jeep and an armoured truck full of government soldiers roared around a corner and through the market. Amos's party looked doubtfully at the town, and back up the road along which they had come. Tortoise gave Amos a look of weary patience. "I think we're supposed to go there," Amos said, his mouth very dry.

"But it's dangerous!" Li'l Massa protested. "Why are you leading us into a war?"

Tortoise nodded impatiently and scratched the ground with a forefoot. "Why do they talk so much?" he asked Amos. "Don't they know they have to follow me?"

"I think we'd better go with him," Amos told the others. Then, as they still hesitated, he told Tortoise, "Go on."

Tortoise started downhill, Amos right behind him. In a moment the others followed. Mr. Stern had scooped up his duck, who had been following freely thus far, and held him under his arm.

The road curved left; the forest shut off their view of the town. Briefly they were in the jungle again. In a clearing to the left, under a huge vine-clad tree, the Brimston Brothers were standing, dressed as tropical explorers in khaki suits and pith helmets. Between them stood a tall, thin, white man in elegant grey-striped trousers and a black frock coat, with a small black bag in his hand. He wore horn-rimmed glasses with a leather strap around the back of his head. Why, thought Amos, he looked almost like Mr. Cartwright, the shop teacher!

The new white man stared at them all, rather indifferently, then focused with more interest on Li'l Massa. He pursed his lips in a calculating manner and drew out a large pocket watch.

"Oh, friend," Norton Brimston called, "at last we've found you—before you could throw away your foolish life."

Hubert Brimston said, "You have to admit that your actions have not exactly been rational. To go all over the world, living the life of a fugitive, when you could have been so comfortable with Dr. Carver here."

Norton Brimston suppressed a laugh. "You were to be his guest ever so long ago. And now he's come to see you, to restore you to reason."

Dr. Carver patted his black bag fondly, then cleared his throat and stepped forward. "Mr. Prendergast," he said in a dry, clinical voice, "how long have you imagined that you were dead?"

Li'l Massa just stared at him. Mr. Stern stepped to his side. "Answer him. You have to speak for yourself."

Li'l Massa looked at Mr. Stern, then at Dr. Carver and his companions. "I *am* dead," he said firmly.

"Come, come." Dr. Carver gave a thin smile. "Many of my patients have that illusion. We'll soon teach you to accept true reality: our own reality. Everyone must come to it in time: if not then, now; if not there, here." He reached into his black bag and took out a thick notebook and a gold fountain pen. The Brimston Brothers crowded each other behind his shoulder, watching the words form with great interest.

"Now," Dr. Carver asked, "how long have you imagined that you were drowned while being abducted by your conniving slaves?"

"I wasn't abducted," Li'l Massa protested, but rather weakly, Amos thought.

Dr. Carver immediately caught the change of tone. "Perhaps you imagined they were your friends, almost your family. You went against all you had been taught, all your deep beliefs—hence your present distress."

"Oh!" Li'l Massa groaned.

"You had the illusion that those niggers really liked you," the doctor continued.

"But they did!" Amos cried. "Usually," he added.

"Aha!" Dr. Carver pounced. "Now I see the source of much of your confusion, Mr. Prendergast. It is this boy, full of jungle lore. His mind is formed by commerce with witch doctors." Dr. Carver flipped through his notebook. "He comes from a family of witch doctors. He may aspire to be one himself."

"Quick," Mr. Stern whispered to Amos. "What is your word for a witch doctor?"

"We call them medicine men, *dibias*," Amos told him. "But I don't believe in them."

"Of course not," Mr. Stern agreed. "But can you call for one now?"

Amos started to shake his head; then he saw Tortoise's dull eye light up with secret amusement. "*I* can't," he told Mr. Stern, "but Tortoise knows how."

Mr. Stern nodded and stepped forward. "Mr. Tortoise, our esteemed leader, could you call a *dibia* for us?" He looked at Tortoise's questioning eye. "You might find it amusing," he added.

Tortoise considered the request. "Why not?" he said at last. He turned his head towards the thick bush and emitted a low, whistling sound.

"You see!" Dr. Carver cried to Li'l Massa. He had been busily writing in his notebook, and now closed it. "They're making mumbo-jumbo, Mr. Prendergast. If you were so ill-advised or foolish as to go to the town below, you'd see how little such jungle superstitions prevail against the loyal and patriotic government troops. Why, what is this?"

From deep in the bush behind the great tree a strange figure approached. He was a tall black man of dignified aspect, though his face was covered with a mask, a very curious mask with large spectacles and a false mustache. He also wore an academic mortarboard, such as Amos had seen at his parents' graduation from medical school. The figure was barefoot, with large rattles around his ankles and chains of bells around his wrists. But he wore a long white laboratory coat, its pockets stuffed with pens and calculators and a large steel retractor. Around his neck was a stethoscope, from which a hairy skin bag hung.

Tortoise regarded him with satisfaction. "How's *that* for a *dibia*?" he asked them all.

The *dibia* advanced, jingling and rattling. He bowed to Tortoise, then advanced courteously towards Dr. Carver. Dr. Carver held his black bag before him defiantly. He stepped towards the *dibia* until they were face to face. "And just where did *you* qualify?" he demanded. "What brings you here to give us the benefit of *your* wisdom?"

The *dibia* showed Dr. Carver the bag hanging from his stethoscope, modestly enough, Amos thought.

"What!" Dr. Carver jeered. "Is that your diploma? From Harvard, perhaps, or Johns Hopkins, or William and Mary? In which witch college did you do your residence?" He laughed at his own pun and repeated, "Which witch college?"

The *dibia* stepped back. The lenses of his spectacles darkened. He slung the end of his stethoscope, which had suddenly grown longer, twice around his neck. Then he gestured above and on either side.

From a branch high above, a large vine came snaking down, just behind Dr. Carver. The doctor didn't see it coming, nor was he aware of it until it wrapped itself around his body and under his arms.

"Help!" he cried piteously, as the vine lifted him in the air. He grasped desperately at his black bag, which fell to the ground, knocking Hubert Brimston's helmet off. Norton Brimston looked up with interest at Dr. Carver, hanging about ten feet above them and uttering shrill cries of terror. "Put me down! Put me down! Oh, oh, oh!" Then he began to gibber senselessly as he rose higher and higher.

The *dibia* stood in front of Amos for a moment, looking deeply into his eyes. He touched his own head, outside the mask, where it was streaked with white paint, and streaked the paint here and there on Amos's face. Then he walked into the bush.

Hubert Brimston picked up Dr. Carver's bag and cleaned it of twigs with a long finger. "The good doctor has a fear of heights that limits his usefulness as a psychiatrist. Pity. But you will meet less civilized gentlemen on your journey, Mr. Prendergast, if you insist on continuing it."

But Tortoise was on his way again, Li'l Massa and all the *Shulamite*'s company following him. Li'l Massa walked ahead to speak to Amos. "Is it true that your parents are witch doctors?"

"They're *real* doctors!" Amos told him indignantly.

Li'l Massa seemed disappointed. "Like Dr. Carver?"

"No sir!"

"That's good," Li'l Massa said. "I liked the *dibia* better. Maybe he could cure my mind. Most of the time, you know, my thoughts were clear. But sometimes I didn't know where I was. On the plantation they said I was crazy just because I sometimes lived in a world of my own, one I liked better." He looked hopefully at Amos, then caught himself and concentrated on the path ahead.

Very soon, the road entered the outskirts of the town, among streets of poor wooden houses such as Amos remembered from the village. They saw only one fine brick house, standing in a garden behind a high iron fence. All its windows were broken, and most of a brick balcony had been blasted off. It was just like the rich man's house in the village, Amos thought, which had never been repaired. Tortoise led them down a broken street, then through others that were in no better case, and into the market they had seen from the hillside.

For the moment, the market was empty. Stalls were deserted, baskets of fruit and yams scattered on the ground. One stall, near a tree, held brightly coloured shirts, many of which had been thrown into the branches.

Near them was the sound of gunfire, growing closer. The soldiers looked to their rifles, but Mr. Stern said to Rufus Palfrey, "Corporal, what will we do? You can't fight all those troops."

Amos spoke up. "We can hide there!" He pointed to a shed in the back of the market, full of concrete blocks. The front of the shed faced a brick wall across an open space from which all the stalls had been cleared, apparently by a truck driving through them. Broken boards were piled at one side of the space.

Amos looked around, trying to control his fear. Would the shed really give them shelter? Or would the gunfire come right through the walls? Could he be shot? And what about his friends? They couldn't die a second time, but they might be in danger of something worse.

"Maybe if we just sit there quietly, quietly, like my Aunt Naomi says, they won't notice us."

"Is that what your aunt says?" Mr. Stern asked with interest.

"Yes, sir."

"And she's likely to know. So what do we do?"

"We should think about other things, if we can. And whatever happens, we mustn't call out."

Everyone but Mr. Stern looked doubtful. Then Tortoise said, "A very fine idea." In a moment he had tucked his head, arms, and legs inside his shell. Then, before their eyes, the markings on his shell faded; the openings sealed over, and where they had seen a living tortoise, there was only a tortoise-shaped green rock.

Toby and Amos ran to the rock and peeped in at the front and sides to see if Tortoise was somehow still there. Rufus Palfrey called them back sternly. "We can't turn into rocks, so we have to do what Amos said. Let's get in that shed and keep quiet."

"And whatever you do," Mr. Stern added, "don't fight them with their own weapons."

They took their places among the concrete blocks, in the darkness of the shed. Rufus Palfrey looked anxiously at the group and distributed them in the most sheltered places. He kept talking. "Now listen, whatever these government soldiers do, you've probably seen worse."

"Likely," Mr. Stern said drily.

"I have too," said Li'l Massa.

Rufus Palfrey looked at him doubtfully. "That's the idea," he encouraged him. "But one thing: you stay with the rest of us. Don't let yourself get separated. Don't try to run off by yourself."

"Run off!" Li'l Massa was incensed. "I'll have you know that a southern gentleman always stays with his servants in time of danger!"

"Oh, Lord," Rufus Palfrey groaned. Then he whispered, "Be quiet now; they're coming."

They heard the sound of many voices and of trucks approaching. Samuel Musgrave nudged Li'l Massa and whispered in his ear. In a moment the white man had opened his Bible to the Psalms, which they both began to read in a stray sunbeam. Samuel Musgrave read more slowly and had to hold up his finger to stop the white man from turning the page too quickly.

But there was time for only one page before the government soldiers came, a troop of them marching to the beat of drums into the market square, led by an officer in dress uniform with many ribbons and medals on his chest. The soldiers formed in ranks along one side of the market square, close to the shed. Some of them hammered a metal stand into the ground, then stuck a large umbrella into it. Canvas chairs were set down beneath the umbrella. Then a sergeant called out, "The foreign dignitaries are coming."

As the government troops watched solemnly, the Brimston Brothers entered, bowed, and took their seats. Drum beats announced the next part of the ceremony.

Eighteen of the soldiers lined up, rifles at half-port. Then other soldiers led in six men dressed in tattered uniforms, their hands tied behind their backs. They left them standing by the wall until the soldiers, three to each captive, shot them.

The men fell without a sound, but the blood that welled out of their bodies looked all too real. Other soldiers dragged the bodies to one side and threw them on the rubble from the market stalls.

Of the next group of six, three cried out in defiance before being shot.

"Who were they?" Hubert Brimston remarked, looking curiously at the pile of bodies.

The officer spread his hands expressively. "Rebels, of course; and such-like scum."

"I see that some were in civilian dress."

"Of course," the officer agreed. "And of doubtful loyalty."

Within the shed, Amos and the others sat as quietly as they could. Samuel Musgrave had taken the Bible to himself and read it with tears rolling down his face. The other soldiers and Pierre Johnson sat with stony faces. Martha cradled Toby in her arms, and Strad put his arm around Amos's shoulder. Mr. Stern said, very quietly, the *Kaddish*, the prayer for the dead.

"This new lot seems quite disturbed," Norton Brimston remarked. Among the next six were two very young men, no more than fourteen, who were crying and struggling to escape and had to be restrained by ropes held by government soldiers on either side. "Why, what is this? What jungle manners do we have here?"

For Amos had run out from the shed and stood between the boys and the firing squad. "You leave them alone!" he cried. "Leave them *all* alone!"

The officer rose to his feet. "Well, a whole delegation," he remarked. For all the others from the shed, Li'l Massa included, had come out and gathered themselves around Amos.

"Why, Mr. Prendergast," Norton Brimston remarked, "have you come to the show?"

Hubert Brimston said, "So, you wish to enter our consciousness now. What do you have to say to us?"

But the sight of the government soldiers had made Li'l Massa speechless. Hubert Brimston turned to the officer. "Sir," he said solemnly, "I appear as an advocate for this wretched man." He indicated Li'l Massa with his elbow. "He fully deserves the full force of your power and your anger."

The glowering officer snapped his fingers and all eighteen soldiers of the firing squad turned towards Li'l Massa, who shrank back against the shed. At a word of command, the squad members fixed bayonets on their rifles and pointed them again at the cowering man.

"See that boy!" Hubert Brimston pointed a long, accusing finger. "Led astray by a boy and an old Jew."

"Oh!" the government soldiers cried indignantly.

The officer called, "A boy! A little professor!"

And the squad echoed, "A little professor!"

"Look at him!" cried the officer. "Standing there, looking on, letting others die in his place. Taking it in. A born observer."

And the firing squad broke up in laughter. They let their rifle butts dangle to the ground and bent and twisted their bodies in strange positions, mocking Amos. Some placed their fingers in their mouths, others placed their hands above their eyes as if they too were wearing glasses. "Oh Professor!" they called, "little Professor Four-eyes! What do you have to teach us today?"

"You go to Hell!" Amos suddenly cried. The soldiers grinned at these wasted words, and the Brimston Brothers broke into loud laughter. "I'll teach you something!" Amos yelled. He scooped up some stones from the ground and began to throw them at the firing squad, forgetting all about their rifles. One or two of them picked up their weapons, but his stones struck their fingers, making them dance and swear.

Martha applauded. "Oh, well done, little David!"

But then the officer rose from his seat, all his medals jingling together, and spoke to Li'l Massa.

"Mr. Prendergast! Don't let these peasant initiatives fool you. My troops will recover soon enough." He looked scornfully at his soldiers, who were still reeling under Amos's well-aimed stones.

But Amos had allies now. *Their* four soldiers had joined in the stone-throwing too, leaving their rifles on the ground. Mr. Stern's duck was flying just above the government soldiers' heads, squawking angrily and flapping his wings in their faces to blind them. Somehow, none of the stones had struck him.

Mr. Stern had not left Li'l Massa's side. He held his arm, looking with admiration on all the fighters on his side.

Hubert Brimston stepped forward. "This is just a pastime," he sneered, spittle flying from his mouth. "Soon these strong, fierce warriors will settle your fellow travellers. Leave them! Come to us! Come to your friends. Come to your true people!"

And the government soldiers, with their officer, cried with one voice, "Go to your people! Go where you belong!"

The sun had disappeared. Black clouds rushed down, from which the shouts of the government soldiers echoed fiercely. Li'l Massa gasped, looked ahead and around. Then Mr. Stern winked at him. Li'l Massa touched Amos's face and said weakly, "But *these* are my friends." Then, with force, "*These* are my friends! *These* are my people!"

In an instant the black cloud vanished. The sun reappeared, some hours farther down the sky than it had been before. The government soldiers immediately set down their weapons, looking disgusted. Two young soldiers stepped behind a bush and could be heard retching.

The officer kept his countenance, despite his disgust. He gathered together all the government soldiers who could control themselves and faced the Brimston Brothers.

"Well, that didn't work very well, did it?" the officer asked them ominously.

The Brimston Brothers gulped. "It's the fault of my brother's misplaced sense of humour," Hubert Brimston pleaded. "It's enough to put anyone off. Can you imagine being exposed to that for all eternity?"

"What happens in all eternity is something the higher authorities will decide," the officer declared. "They won't like lending their good troops for no purpose. We'll go see them now, *gentlemen.*"

And the government soldiers picked up their rifles, formed around the Brimston Brothers, and marched them off. "Move on, Whitey!" one soldier cried. "Paleface, your time has come!" cried another. The officer just smiled and let these lapses of discipline pass.

Amos's group watched them depart in silence. At last, Tortoise spoke. "They certainly don't make devils like they used to. It's a wonder your world's not a better place. But come," he added, "now we must go to the sea."

Tortoise led the way out of the market. He breathed deeply and started to hum to himself. Pierre Johnson caught the tune and began to sing the words to it, an old sailor's ballad:

At the end of the journey
Comes the sea:
A grave for you,
A cradle for me.
We'll rock there together
Until the Last Day,
When the spirits fly up
In the foam and the spray.

He forgot the other words, but walked on after Tortoise, and the others followed after, savouring the fresh salty air.

CHAPTER TWELVE

Museum Stories

Sure enough, the sea was not so far away—just past the marketplace and the cracked sidewalks along the main street, where grass was springing up again, and the frightened, hopeful eyes of the townspeople looked out from behind broken windows. Somewhere, a radio began to play. Then there was the sound of rich violin music that grew louder as they approached the seafront.

There, on the broken boardwalk, fishermen were once more mending their nets and families were sitting quietly together to watch the purple and gold sunset.

They passed in front of a seaside hotel, once a fine, wide building, though its façade was much pitted with bullet holes. A sign with fresh paint read, "Wagstaff Hotel: the Master of Falcon Island." Waiters were sweeping broken glass from the patio and setting out tables. Pierre Johnson looked at the sign with interest, but soon his eyes were fixed on his boat, which was moored to a rickety wharf by a golden cable. The *Shulamite* was still painted black, but a glowing black, over a rich gold ground. Its keel was no wider than before, but its deck spread out on each side like wings, Amos thought. He was sure this boat could take to the air and fly once it was out to sea!

"Man, they really did some work on her!" the captain said. "I don't know where we're going, but I know she'll get us there."

On the poop deck a Stradivarius violin hung in the air, playing itself with a silver bow. Its melody called Li'l Massa aboard, with a new spring in his step.

Mr. Stern gently stroked his duck and tossed the faithful bird into the air. But it did not land on the *Shulamite*, as he had expected: it flew past and out to sea, its wings growing ever stronger and longer.

Then everyone but Amos stepped aboard the boat. Pierre Johnson was so keen to go that he hardly said goodbye. Samuel Musgrave looked as pious as could be expected; Josiah Stone talked of meeting his mother; Jefferson White shook his head and remarked, "I hope it won't be dull after all that's happened."

"There'll be things you never dreamed of," Samuel Musgrave rebuked him.

"That I have to see," said Jefferson White doubtfully.

Old Mr. Stern was calm. "Now I'll get the answers to a few questions. I hope I like what I get." He laid his hand on Amos's head for the last time and turned away to hide his tears.

Strad and Martha were happy, of course. "I hope the trip don't last too long," Strad whispered to Amos. "I'm still not sure how to deal with Li'l Massa."

"You'll manage," Martha told him. "You did for long enough."

Toby said, "I wish you were coming too," but his father shook his head. "He'll have to wait for his own time," he said.

Toby's main attention was on some fine fishing gear mounted along the stern rail. "I just can't wait to see what I'll catch with that!" Toby said, brightening up.

"Say," he told Amos, "when you get there, I'll really be able to show you around."

Amos tried to smile, and he and Tortoise watched the *Shulamite* sail off. The sea was as blue as the sky, and the horizon melted away, so that by the time the boat disappeared they couldn't tell if it was in water or air. To the end, they could still see Mr. Stern's duck hovering over it.

"Well," Tortoise said, "that will be a new one for my biographers. And how fortunate that you have just the artistic talent I need."

"I have?" said Amos.

"So I've been told," Tortoise informed him. "Now I have to take you to my Museum."

Tortoise led Amos along the seashore to the end of the boardwalk, then up a steep rocky path to a cave high above the surf. As they proceeded, Amos noticed that Tortoise was growing smaller—he was no more than three feet long now—though still much larger than when he'd opened the door to the House of the Good Spirits.

Tortoise was panting by the time they reached the cave. He caught his breath and announced proudly, "And here we are!"

Amos stepped inside and looked around. The setting sun lit up the walls of the light, roomy cave so that he could see the smooth sun-warmed stone walls, and lichens growing on them here and there, and a few cracks. But there was little else. "Did you say this was a museum?" he asked Tortoise politely, for the vain animal had an uncommonly self-satisfied look.

"A museum in its purest form," Tortoise told him. "A splendid setting for one gem, and potential home for many more." Amos followed the direction of Tortoise's head to a small alcove in one corner, where a figure was engraved. He walked closer and saw a design of a tortoise with a large gourd on his back, preparing to climb a palm tree.

"Is that the Calabash of Wisdom?" he asked.

"The very same," Tortoise said proudly. "As it really was when I began to climb that tree. Of course, I carried the Calabash on my back from the first; I knew enough not to put it on my front, the way some people said I did. Could you climb a tree with a burden like that on *your* front? My devotees—there is a modest Tortoise cult—wanted to set the matter right and cut the figure there long ago; you can see some of the original pigments in the rocks."

Amos looked more closely and saw that the Calabash was open. "And did you store all the wisdom of the world in that Calabash?"

"Alas, no," Tortoise sighed. "Wisdom is lighter than air; who can seize it? As soon as I opened the stopper to add more, what I had already gathered flew away. That wisdom is still in the air, waiting.

"But we're wasting time," he added. "The reason I brought you here is that my walls are too bare. I understand you can draw, so I ask you—before I show you the way back home again—to illustrate my legends on the walls of my cave."

"All of them?" Amos asked in dismay.

"As many as you find space for," Tortoise said generously. "Those that you don't remember, I will. Here is a box of new pencils," he added.

Fortunately, the smooth stone walls of the cave took pencil strokes well. Even more fortunately, Tortoise appreciated Amos's artistic abilities; he didn't object even when the pictures showed some of his bad points.

First, Amos drew Tortoise's competition with Rabbit, as to which would offer the greatest hospitality. He only drew the funny part, in which Tortoise pretended to be cooked in soup as a dish for Rabbit; he left out the part about Rabbit really being cooked and eaten by Tortoise, and the later terrible vengeance of Rabbit's wife, who tricked Tortoise and made him kill his own wife and children.

Next, he drew the story of how Tiger had insulted Tortoise by hiring all the animals but him to work on his farm; and how Tortoise had distracted all the other animals with music and dancing so that they couldn't work at all. These pictures took up all of one section of a wall. While Amos drew, Tortoise scrabbled back and forth watching Tiger and the other animals appear, and hissing and whistling in admiration.

Then Amos showed Tortoise falsely accused of the murder of Beetle, his housemate, and running and hiding in river swamps. "Yes," Tortoise said, looking at the trees and mangroves Amos had sketched on the wall. "It was just like that!"

Tortoise even let Amos draw the terrible story of his treachery during the war between the beasts and the birds, when he invited the birds to a great feast, then trapped them in the banquet hall and burned them alive. "If it weren't for those silly birds," he told Amos, "I might not be serving out my time as a lowly messenger between the different worlds." But Amos thought he really didn't seem to be as sorry as all that.

Tortoise rattled around the cave and watched the walls fill up with Amos's pictures, and Amos had to admit that he had never drawn faster or better. Now there was just room to draw again the story of how Tortoise carried the message about death to God. But rather than have Tortoise pass through that same old bush, this time Amos drew a picture of the old house, the House of the Good Spirits, which he himself had entered so long ago.

Tortoise applauded the house. "You have a real feeling for spaces," he announced, and Amos saw that he had grown smaller still. He began yet another drawing of

Tortoise, low on the wall, near the floor. The fine lines of the drawing burned into Amos's brain so that he had to close his eyes for a minute....

Someone was shaking his shoulder. "I told you he'd be here, Miss Naomi," Lester Prewitt said. "He must have fallen asleep."

Amos sat up. His hand still held a pencil, but it was pressed against a board. On the board he had drawn a picture of Tortoise. It was dark outside, but in the beam of Mr. Prewitt's flashlight he was sure the tortoise on the board winked at him before becoming still for ever.

Lester Prewitt was standing by him, trying to help him rise, but he got up by himself. Naomi opened the door. Moonlight fell over her shoes, over the gravel path, and on the lake. "Are you back with us yet?" Lester Prewitt asked.

Amos shook his head. "I guess so," he mumbled.

He stepped outside, then heard Lester Prewitt exclaim, "It looks like the door from the shed to the house has been opened. There's a clearing in the leaves."

Amos and Naomi came back to look. It was true: the dry leaves on the floor were shoved aside, as if the door had recently been opened outward. Lester Prewitt tried to open it again. "Nope," he said, "locked tight as a drum. One of the Murdochs must have been by. You're lucky he didn't catch you."

"What time is it?" Amos asked.

"So, you can talk now," Naomi said. She had been holding him by the arm, and now she put her arm around his shoulders. "It's almost nine."

"Oh, gosh!" Amos said. "I was supposed to go to the Bidcups' house. Are Mother and Daddy mad at me?"

Naomi chuckled. "You're lucky again! They're still at the hospital. They never did get to that big dinner party."

Amos shook his head stupidly. "They didn't?"

"You're still not all here, sonny," Lester Prewitt said from Amos's other side. "Have you been dreaming in there?"

"Am I still dreaming now?" Amos wondered. Lester Prewitt and Naomi laughed.

"*Now* you're awake, or almost," Naomi said, "so let me tell you about the trouble you escaped, thanks to your busy parents. Just after you left I got a phone call from Mrs. Bidcup. Of course they were expecting me, she said. She had thought I'd be coming along with you. So I went by the library to pick you up."

"It was closed."

"That's what I saw. So I went to the Bidcups', and you hadn't come. Not to make a big fuss, I said you had another errand; so we waited. Some other folk had shown up, but no one from the hospital. It seems a government committee is coming to look them over and Mr. Bidcup and that Dr. Baillie and all the other doctors had to get everything prepared just so. So," she laughed, "those of us who weren't so important got to know each other.

"There was a girl there from your class, Dr. Bellechasse's daughter."

"Juliette?"

"That's the one." Naomi smiled. "She was disappointed when you didn't turn up. But mostly, I talked to Mrs. Bidcup. She said you were getting on fine, better than you told me. She knew all about that Mr. Cartwright. Did you know that?"

"No. I didn't tell her anything."

"Well, someone did. She knew what he said, word for word. She told me, 'I got him sorted out on that. I let him know that if I hear of any more such talk, I'll really clean his clock!' "

Naomi looked at him with amusement. "You thought she was as dumb as her husband, didn't you? She's a smart lady. She has a better job than he does, too." She shook her head. "Women have to put up with a lot!"

"Are Mother and Daddy at her house now?" Amos asked.

"I doubt it. I came out because you still hadn't come, and I said I'd look out for you and call in. I found Mr. Prewitt on the street and he had an idea you might be here. What's that on your head?" Naomi shone Mr. Prewitt's flashlight on Amos's face. "Chalk marks? Where'd you get those? They look like a *dibia*'s decoration. Here." She took a handkerchief and wiped them off.

They had walked past the old house, by the granite boulder, and up the path towards Main Street. In the house by Driftwood Fashions a number of people were sitting around a large table, talking busily. "What's going on in there?" Lester Prewitt muttered.

Amos had stopped to watch the faces of the family in the house, so that by the time he reached Main Street, Lester Prewitt was already looking at the typewritten notice on the front door. She and Mr. Prewitt moved aside to let him read the notice too: "Due to the death of our beloved grandfather, David Stern, Driftwood Fashions will be closed until next Monday."

Both Naomi and Lester Prewitt were silent as they walked down Main Street. Mr. Prewitt wiped his eyes with a red handkerchief. "He knew this was going to happen; I could tell when we said goodbye the last time, he gave me such a smile and thanked me for everything I had brought him. I think he meant you, too," he added to Amos. He blew his nose loudly. "He was a smart man. I'll never meet one like him again."

Naomi was sniffling a little. "You liked him, didn't you?" she asked Amos. He nodded. "He seemed so lonely, with that family of his," Naomi continued.

"You never knew what he'd say next," Lester Prewitt said.

"That's right," said Amos.

"You noticed that too?" Lester Prewitt shook his head. "It's a real shame you didn't get to know him better."

Amos started to say that he had got to know Mr. Stern pretty well, but stopped. "Stern means 'star'," he said instead. "He told me that."

"That's right," Lester Prewitt said. "He used to make a little joke about that. 'David of the Star', he called himself."

Naomi called the Bidcups' from a phone booth and then reported, "Your folks are still not there, and the party's over. In fact, Mrs. Bidcup's gone to drive some of the other children home."

As they approached the museum, a car travelling east on Main Street slowed, then stopped. Mrs. Bidcup got out of the driver's seat and Juliette Bellechasse from the other door. "Well, my last passenger asked me to come this way," Mrs. Bidcup said. "She figured they might have found you, Amos. Where were you?"

"We found him sound asleep by the old Murdoch place," Lester Prewitt said, before Amos could speak.

"Did you, now? By our local haunted house. I hope you didn't go inside."

Amos hung his head. "The door was locked."

"Well, I should hope so. That means you tried it, though. Let's just keep that to ourselves, shall we?" Mrs. Bidcup looked at Lester Prewitt, who nodded. "You too, Juliette."

"Of course." Juliette turned up her nose, but she also walked a little to the side so that Amos could talk to her alone. Naomi and Mrs. Bidcup sat down for a moment on a stone bench across from the museum and the city hall.

"You really couldn't get into the house?" Juliette asked.

"I told you, the door was locked."

"But you were there a long time."

"I fell asleep," Amos said, feeling foolish. But then he added, "Boy, did I have a dream!" He fell silent, remembering.

"Well," Juliette added after a while, "will you tell me about it? Or don't you remember it? I forget most of my dreams."

"I remember it all. Maybe I'll tell you tomorrow. But I want to sleep on it first." He laughed as a new thought struck him. "That Mr. Prendergast, the one they called Li'l Massa, he wasn't so dumb after all. Maybe he was crazy but he sure wasn't stupid: he knew all the time that he was in a dream."

"What?" Juliette demanded.

Amos shook his head. "I'll tell you tomorrow," he said again.

"What are you children so serious about?" Mrs. Bidcup called. "Juliette, we have to go. What is it, Mr. Prewitt?"

For Lester Prewitt, who had been looking across the street, now suddenly ran into the alley beside the museum. "I've got you, you little devils!" he cried. He came out below the streetlight holding Norman Glanders by the collar with one hand and Henry Stiggs with the other. Norman struggled so hard that his collar tore, but before he could get away, Mr. Prewitt grasped him by the neck. He pushed both boys against the museum wall and stood before them, daring them to run. "Now, button up!" he told them. They zipped up their trousers, turning aside suddenly when they saw Mrs. Bidcup.

"You were going to piss on my museum wall!" Mr. Prewitt declared.

"Honest, Lester," Norman Glanders began, in tears.

"Mr. Prewitt to you, laddie!"

"Honest, Mr. Prewitt," said Henry Stiggs, "we just had to go, and every other place was shut."

"You saw me standing here. You could have asked to be let in." Mr. Prewitt had calmed down now. "Do you still have to go?"

Both boys nodded.

"Come on, then. It's lucky for you I caught you before and not after." He opened the door and showed the boys in, adding, "It's a museum, not a latrine. You'd better learn the difference." He looked across the street, said, "Excuse the language," and followed the boys into the museum.

Mrs. Bidcup tried not to laugh. "Look at that moon. It's a pity to go in, but I have to take Juliette home. But wait…is that the colonel sitting there?"

Sure enough, the moon shone on the white hair of Colonel Murdoch, who was sitting on the city hall steps.

"Come over and join us, Colonel," Mrs. Bidcup called. The colonel smiled, crossed the street, and sat on the bench too.

The museum door opened and the two boys came out, followed by Mr. Prewitt. "You go home now," he told them.

"Okay," Norman said. "Thanks, Mr. Prewitt."

"Is that all?"

"What?" Then Henry poked Norman and nodded across the street. "Oh. Good night, Mrs. Bidcup," Norman said. "Good night, everybody."

"Good night, everybody," Henry echoed. Everyone called good night in turn. The boys started down Main Street, very quietly.

"Well," Mrs. Bidcup said to Amos, "I bet you don't have any more trouble with those two."

"I'm not worried about them," Amos said and added, without thinking, "I stood up to the government soldiers!"

"What?" Mrs. Bidcup was looking at him very curiously.

"He's still a little sleepy," Naomi said quickly.

Mrs. Bidcup nodded. "Come on, Juliette. But can I give you two a ride home, Mrs. Obi?"

"We'll just walk, thank you," Naomi said. "It's such a fine night."

After Mrs. Bidcup and Juliette had driven away, Naomi walked up and down the street, busy with her own thoughts. Amos sat on the bench beside Mr. Prewitt. The wind from the lake was beginning to grow chill.

"I guess we should all be in bed," Lester Prewitt remarked. The colonel nodded glumly. "Do you have far to go, Colonel?"

"Not far enough."

"You don't sound happy."

"I don't like it there. It's a boarding-house, you know."

"No, I didn't know."

"That's what it is. The people there," the colonel added reflectively, "have no sense of history."

Lester Prewitt nodded. "I can see you wouldn't feel much at home, in that case."

The colonel turned his head to the museum. "I feel right at home here, though." He added, "You sleep in the museum, don't you?"

Lester Prewitt nodded again.

"I guessed right," the colonel said happily.

"I have a cot in the basement," Lester Prewitt told him. "To watch the furnace. But there's a couch on the third floor, where no one goes, that you could use."

"Do you think so?"

"Mr. Hicks wouldn't mind, if we broke it to him gently."

Naomi had approached the bench. "We have to go home now, Amos." She shook the colonel's hand and suddenly kissed Mr. Prewitt's cheek. "A friend died," she told the colonel.

He nodded gravely. "Sometimes that brings people closer together." This seemed to bring up thoughts of his family. "You know," he said, "I had thought of going to that old house by the lake. It's Murdoch property. But it might not be comfortable. What is it you call it? The House of the Good Spirits?"

"That's it."

"A good name. No, we'd better leave it to the spirits." The two old men chuckled together.

Amos almost told them that the spirits were no longer there, but decided it would make too long a story. Instead, he just said goodnight. As he and Naomi passed the old fort they saw Colonel Murdoch and Lester Prewitt walking together to the museum.

ACKNOWLEDGEMENTS

The following works were consulted for the various folk tales:

African Folktales Roger D. Abrahams. Pantheon Books, New York, 1983. (The story of the skull in the bush.)

The Calabash of Wisdom and other Igbo Stories Romanus Egudu. NOK Publishers International, New York, London, Lagos, Enugu, 1973. (All of the Tortoise stories.)

Folk Tales of French Canada. Edith Fowke. NC Press, Toronto, 1982. ("Fearless Pierre" and "The Chasse Galerie"; the two direct quotes are from this book.)

Other source material:

Biafra: (Volume 1) Selected Speeches with Journals of Events. C. Odumegwu Ojukwu. Harper and Row, New York, Evanston, and London, 1969.

The Blacks in Canada: A History. Robin W. Winks. Yale University Press/McGill-Queen's Press, New Haven and Montreal, 1971.

Blacks in Deep Snow: Black Pioneers in Canada. Colin A. Thomson. J.M. Dent and Sons (Canada), Don Mills, Ontario, 1979.

Booze, Boats and Billions: Smuggling Liquid Gold! C.W. Hunt. McClelland and Stewart, Toronto, 1988.

The Freedom-Seekers: Blacks in Early Canada. Daniel G. Hill. Book Society of Canada, Agincourt, Ontario, 1981.

Great Slave Narratives. Selected and Introduced by Arna Bontemps. Beacon Press, Boston, 1969.

The Man Died: Prison Notes. Wole Soyinka. Spectrum Books, Ibadan, Owerri, Kaduna, 1972.

Sunset in Biafra. Elechi Amadi. Heinemann, London, Ibadan, Nairobi, Lusaka, 1973.